LAST CHANCE CHRISTMAS

AJ WYNN

ALSO BY AJ WYNN

Willowbrooke
The Other Side

LAST CHANCE CHRISTMAS

AJ WYNN

*To everyone who wanted more of Chance and Violet...
it turns out I wasn't ready to let them go yet, either.*

Thank you for your kind words of encouragement.

Enjoy!

AUTHOR'S NOTE

Last Chance Christmas is a cozy holiday mystery romance
novella with spice, following an established couple.

It can be read as a standalone but will be
greatly enhanced if preceded by *The Other Side*.

 # HARPER HOUSE 

Winter Revelry

Sunday
DECEMBER 19

AFTERNOON TEA

Ladies only. Formal tea attire requested.
All proceeds support the Havenwell Collective.

Monday
DECEMBER 20

BENEFIT CONCERT

Featuring the Astoria Quartet.
All proceeds support the Starling Foundation.

Tuesday
DECEMBER 21

CHARITY AUCTION

Silent auction and holiday marketplace to precede live auction.
All proceeds support the Elmwood Society of the Arts.

Wednesday
DECEMBER 22

CHILDREN'S FESTIVAL

Refreshments provided. Guests of all ages are welcome.
All proceeds support the Roberts Children's Foundation.

Thursday
DECEMBER 23

MASQUERADE BALL

Black-tie attire. Masks provided.
All proceeds support Montgomery Preparatory School.

Friday
DECEMBER 24

DONOR DINNER

By exclusive invite only.

HARPER HOUSE

PORTLAND, ME

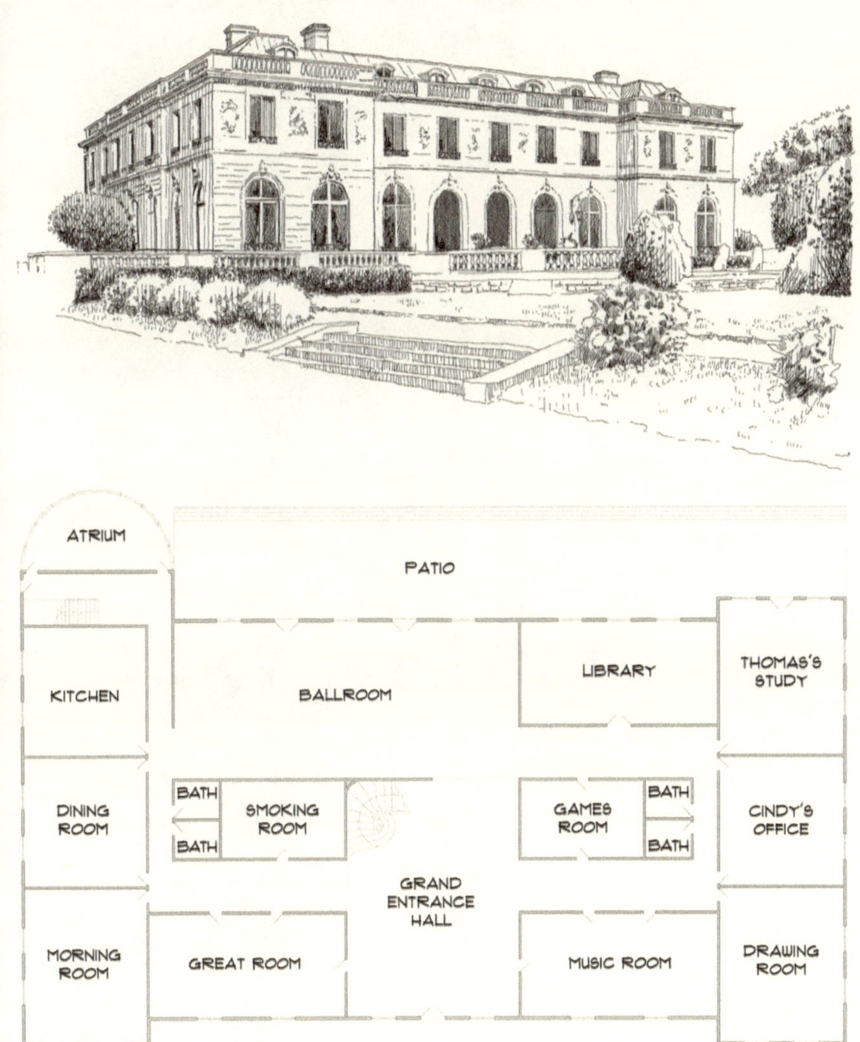

GROUND FLOOR PLAN

FRIDAY, DECEMBER 17

CHAPTER 1

"You look awfully miserable for someone who just finished her last class before the holiday break."

I grumbled at Lenny, the beleaguered Montgomery Prep head chef, and also my closest friend at work, across the prep table, where he was putting away utensils, tidying up for the kitchen to be closed for the next month.

"When does he get back?"

"Tomorrow." I sighed morosely, sinking onto the table, letting my chin rest on my forearm.

Chance had gotten permission to leave for the holiday break a week early, to attend a photographer's showcase in Edinburgh to accept an award. I was so fucking proud of him, I thought my heart might burst.

I'd requested time off to go with him, but Headmistress Jones had refused, as there were already a handful of other teachers who were leaving for their vacations early. She couldn't allow the school to be too short-staffed.

She'd been kind enough to allow us to continue seeing each other while working as teachers at our elite boarding school, despite the code of conduct, which prohibited fraternization. So I didn't exactly want to press my luck with her.

It was the first time since Daniel's funeral the spring before that we'd been apart for more than a day, and I hadn't anticipated how much I would crumble without Chance. I hated feeling weak or reliant on him, after years of being perhaps hyper-independent. But I loved him, and he had become a stabilizing force in my life. Without him, I was grumpy, lonely, and more anxious than I'd felt in a very long time.

"Think you'll manage?" Lenny joked.

I stuck my tongue out at him, garnering a chuckle.

Lenny and I had become fast friends during my first year teaching, and the curmudgeonly cook had reluctantly taken me under his wing. After all the awful things that had happened the year before, he'd become even more protective, but definitely retained his salty rhetoric.

"Any plans during break?" I asked, tilting my head to one side to rest my cheek on my arm as I peered up at him.

"Heading down to Georgia to meet my new grandbaby." He smiled.

I couldn't help but mirror his response. "That sounds wonderful."

He nodded in agreement. "You?"

The sigh I gave this time was more dreamy. "Absolutely nothing."

Lenny chuckled.

"I think we'll just stay in the apartment for the next month, only leaving for groceries, and binge-watch every single TV show we can find." I decided to leave out the part where we'd be tangled up in each other.

That was what I was most looking forward to, as our never-ending schoolwork and added commute often left both of us too tired for much romance, despite the fact that Chance and I continued to harbor a very healthy desire for one another.

The holidays were a bittersweet time of year for me. I'd grown up in poverty and my mother, despite her best efforts, had struggled with depression for as long as I could remember. Some Christmases were better than others and she had tried so hard, but the last one I'd spent at home, over a decade ago, had resulted in me discovering my boyfriend had been having an affair with my best friend.

Needless to say, I hadn't been home for the holidays since. Instead, I'd chosen to develop my own set of traditions that included comfort foods, nostalgic holiday movies, and now cozying up with Chance. I was excited to evolve my Christmas traditions to include new things that made him happy.

It was nice to have something to look forward to at all. Chance had given that to me.

"You better get going if you don't want to get stuck in traffic on the way home," Lenny hedged.

Traffic in our neck of the woods amounted to having to wait behind a couple cars on the one-lane highway that connected the school to the closest town about twenty minutes away, or worst-case, getting stuck behind a slow-moving truck. So I took that as my cue to get lost, as Lenny was clearly trying to get rid of me so he could leave himself.

I rounded the corner of the kitchen prep table and wrapped Lenny in a tight hug. "Merry Christmas, Lenny."

"Merry Christmas, Violet." He pulled me in a little closer. And when we separated, he told me to drive safely before sending me on my way.

The scene outside was nothing but picturesque. Bright white snow glittered in the setting sunlight, twinkling amongst the tall evergreen trees. Normally I loved the lead-up to the holidays, but they'd felt lackluster since I'd dropped Chance off at the airport a week prior.

Even driving home made my chest ache for him. He always drove us, holding my hand across the console the whole way, or occasionally squeezing my knee if he was feeling particularly cheeky.

I blushed thinking about how *those* drives led to more the second we got home.

Pulling into the driveway of our little rental house, I heaved another sigh, not wanting to go into a quiet and empty house, although it would be the last night I'd have to sleep alone for a while, I hoped.

Chance would be lucky if I'd let him out of bed for the next week, once he was back. I sent him a naughty text saying as much, and felt dejected when it wasn't immediately read. Edinburgh was only four hours ahead, so he should have still been awake.

My breath began to fog in the car as the cold from outside seeped in. I groaned, grabbing my bag and slinging it over my shoulder as I exited the vehicle and made my way inside, where the only thing that greeted me was the warmth of our cozy space.

Heck, between finals and his travel, we hadn't even had a chance to put up any decorations or to go find our first Christmas tree, even though I usually had decorations up promptly on Thanksgiving. I'd thought about suggesting adding an annual ornament exchange to the tradition list.

Fuck, it even smells like him in here, I thought to myself as I frowned, chucking my bag to the ground before toeing off my dirty boots and hanging my coat in the entryway. I dropped the keys on their designated hook before rounding the corner into the kitchen to forage for something in the fridge to make for dinner.

I froze.

Leaning casually against the counter was Chance.

How was it fair that he was impossibly more handsome than the last time I'd seen him, wiping errant tears from my eyes as I'd dropped him off at the airport? With one leg crossed over the other in dark jeans, he looked like a tall, lean god.

His blue-grey eyes crinkled at the edges as he smiled, pleased with my reaction.

"Hello, muse."

Upon hearing his voice, my shock immediately abated and I ran to him, all but jumping into his arms, wrapping my legs around his hips.

"You're home!" I pulled his mouth to mine before he could respond.

Chance wasted no time in drawing me in. Feeling his warm hand at my nape, pulling me closer, smelling his aftershave, tasting coffee on his lips, I felt like I was home...my other half having been reconnected to my soul.

"I missed you..." I sighed, between kisses.

"I couldn't stay away." He grinned, before perching me on the kitchen island, allowing him to use both hands, instead of having to support me with one. "Even though you hate surprises." Chance chuckled against me, his fingers already working to remove my pants.

"I *do* hate surprises." I laughed, grabbing Chance's face to bring his lips back to mine.

I loved it when Chance's kisses were hungry and desperate, and you couldn't get more hungry and desperate than after having been apart for a week. I felt every moment of our separation in the rhythm of his mouth pushing and pulling against mine, tugging at every last strand of my sanity with each stroke.

He withdrew from me with a pained huff, frustrated with the distraction, while he decided to go after what he really wanted from me.

"Lie back." His voice was commanding and gruff.

Normally I abhorred demands, but when they came from Chance, I was helpless. I complied without arguing, even lifting my hips as he slid my slacks and panties off, using his foot to shove them to the side so he could kneel in front of me, where my core was level with his face.

"I want you inside…" I whined, rubbing my legs together to alleviate the pressure building between them, ignoring the goosebumps that had erupted along my bare skin.

"You'll take what I give you," Chance growled, his tone husky and lined with impatience.

This was all part of the game we played. I'd talk back and he'd pretend to be annoyed with my impetuousness, while we both knew he fucking loved it, just as much as I loved it when he ordered me around.

I yelped in surprise when, with gruff hands, Chance yanked me to the edge of the kitchen island, my legs teetered precariously over the edge, barely allowing me to balance, until he hooked each of my knees over his shoulders.

I moaned as his big warm hands trailed up my thighs, his touch now gentle as he coaxed me to spread open for him. I knew he'd probably find me already on my way to being soaked. His impatience never failed to turn me on.

Demonstrating said impatience, one moment his warm breath was fanning over my outer folds and the next his teeth were nipping at my clit. I let out a short shriek of surprise at the sensation, my hips bucking in response, but he was holding on to my hips tightly, ensuring I stayed in place while he continued to use his devilish mouth to nip, suck, and lick me right to the brink.

Chance's ravenous appetite knew no bounds. He reached for every little bit of me that he could get, reveling in every keening whimper he elicited from my lips and devouring me whole with every stroke of his tongue.

But just when I was about to crest, he pulled away.

I released a strangled cry at the loss.

"Not yet," Chance ground out as he stood, carefully guiding my legs as they slid off his shoulders. He hooked them around his hips, so I could retain my balance between him and the kitchen counter. With hooded eyes that were solely focused on me, he unzipped and pulled his cock from the confines of his jeans.

His hand stroked up and down, once, then twice, and when he began the third time, I resorted to begging. "Please," I pleaded, squirming against the cold countertop, a frown marring my face.

He smiled at my discomfort and need. I reached out for him, but was unable to raise my back from the counter without risking injury.

"Is it awful that I love seeing you so desperate?" He half laughed.

"Yes," I snapped. "I asked nicely." My voice came out more of a whine than I had intended.

Chance took a step forward, rubbing the head of his dick against my clit, sending a pulse of need through my entire body. I threw my head back against the counter and moaned.

"You hate how much you need me." I didn't have to see Chance to know he was smiling.

"Stop torturing me..." I cried. "I haven't seen you in a week." I looked up, meeting Chance's bemused eyes. "I need you...please..."

Chance leaned over me, placing a soft kiss at my throat. "I love you too," he whispered as he slowly began to slide into me.

A low groan rumbled through his chest and against mine as he seated himself within me. I could only sigh in relief at the fullness and pressure I constantly felt the loss of when he wasn't inside me.

With my legs slung high on Chance's hips, he was able to go deeper than usual, hitting places he rarely found, instantly reigniting my climb toward a climax while he thrust against me in a steady rhythm, knowing exactly what I needed before even I did.

"Such a good girl," Chance whispered against my throat. "...my sweet girl..."

I surrendered to the movement of our hips, losing myself in the feel of his body rocking against mine and chasing my orgasm, which didn't take long to catch, crashing over me like a tidal wave, halting my breath in my lungs for a moment as I let it wash over me, my body left trembling in its wake.

Chance groaned into my neck, sucking on the same spot he'd been focusing on, as my body clenched around him. A moment later his pumping became erratic before he found his own release, finishing inside me, thanks to my IUD.

"Fuck..." Chance's body relaxed over mine, his cock still buried inside me. "I needed that." He looked up at me. "I needed you."

I reached out tentative fingers to brush his hair from his face. "I love you." My voice was as soft and pliant as my body.

A grin wreathed his face. "I love you too."

CHAPTER 2

It still amazed me, even after almost a year of being together, officially, how easy things continued to be with Chance. The more I opened up, the more secure he made me feel. I was still working through a lot of my own insecurities, but I continued seeing my therapist, Dr. Short, weekly, and Chance was there with me every step of the way.

The insidious voice in my head that told me I wasn't worthy of the love I was receiving—that everything with Chance was too good to be true—was getting quieter each day, although occasionally rearing its ugly head to pull me into a bit of a spiral.

As Dr. Short reminded me, I was worthy, and instead of believing all of the goodness around me was going to disappear, she would ask me to think about what it would be like if it didn't, and to allow myself to envision that future, even if I found it difficult to stop assuming the worst would happen.

"What if all of those traumatic things had to happen before to allow you to appreciate and cherish what you have now?" Dr. Short had asked me during my most recent session. "If you're spiritual, or believe in karma, or just the power of the universe, what if it's simply now your turn to have harmony in your life?"

So when Chance pulled me into the shower with him, I told myself to stay in the moment and to appreciate him and our relationship exactly as it was...rather than dwelling on how empty I felt while he was gone and how much worse it would feel if things ever came to an end between us. Because things between us weren't just good, they were amazing. And that was something to celebrate.

"You're so quiet, Violet." Chance traced a fingertip along the curve of my bottom lip while we cuddled in bed after a quick dinner and a third round of sex. "It worries me when you're quiet," he said softly.

"I'm just so glad you caught an earlier flight." I nuzzled against his chest. "I didn't like being here alone."

"I triple-checked the security system before I left and was monitoring everything in the app—"

"No." I shook my head. "I just missed you," I clarified.

Chance's expression relaxed, then morphed into one that meant he was preparing to tease me. "What did you get up to all by yourself in the apartment?" His fingers continued to skim over my skin, venturing first down the column of my throat, then to my clavicle, then began gentle circles around my breast. "You must have been so lonely without someone to attend to your needs."

I snorted a laugh. "You're the one chasing me around," I accused him, and rightfully so.

"You like being chased." He leaned down, taking my nipple in his mouth and smiling against my breast when I gasped at the sensation.

"Only when it's you..." I breathed through the pulse I felt at my core as a result of his ministrations.

His phone went off suddenly, the vibration reverberating loudly on the nightstand.

Chance groaned, separating himself from his body to turn and dismiss the call, but when I saw him deflate, I peeked over his shoulder.

It was his mom.

"Answer it," I told him.

"But—" He looked back at me, then down at my breasts, then back up to me.

I rolled my eyes. "My boobs will still be here in two minutes." I scoffed.

With another groan, he picked up the call, immediately putting it on speaker. "Hi, Mom."

"Hi, honey," Cindy's sweet voice came over the speaker.

"Violet's here too." He glanced up at me.

"Hello, dear," she offered sincerely. "Does that mean you're already back home?"

"Yeah, I was able to get on an earlier flight."

"Oh, wonderful," she continued. "I was just calling to ask what time you'll both be arriving tomorrow so your room is ready for you."

Chance's eyebrows shot up as he stared at me in alarm. "Tomorrow?" he questioned, his voice pitched higher than normal.

"Yes, for the Winter Revelry," she stated matter-of-factly.

"Winter Revelry?" I whispered in confusion to Chance.

Perhaps sensing our bafflement in the sudden silence, Cindy provided more context. "I texted you about it in October, honey." Her tone grew slightly more stern. "You promised you'd attend. My numbers will all be off if you aren't here."

Chance gave me a beseeching look, then pressed mute on the phone. "I don't remember agreeing to anything." He shook his head, anticipating I'd be upset with him. "I told her we'd go to the New Year's party, but that's all."

"Tell her you forgot and ask her to resend the information," I instructed him, trying not to let any frustration seep through my tone. I knew this was a misunderstanding and that he hadn't done anything intentionally.

"Can you resend me the invite, please?" he asked his mom, after taking her off mute.

Both our phones buzzed a moment later.

Chance's mouth fell open. "A week!?" he said in a hushed whisper meant only for my ears.

"I'm sorry, I should have sent the original invite to Violet as well," Cindy apologized as I read through the week-long schedule of events. "It's just that, with your father and I deciding to relocate to the penthouse permanently so we can open the estate up to the public for tours and events, it's my last chance to really enjoy these events while the house still feels like our home."

I sighed, my plans of staying in bed all week with Chance evaporating in front of me and yet another year of Christmas Eve traditions pushed along the wayside.

RIP Grammy Caitlin's mac and cheese.

And perhaps I was annoyed with the situation, but I could tell it was important to Cindy, and I understood this was part of the deal if I wanted to be with Chance...to be a part of his life...a part of his family...

She'd told me about how all the proceeds from the estate being opened up were going to benefit the charities she worked with, I just hadn't spoken to her as much in the fall, so it was easy to see how things could have gotten mixed up.

"What time would you like us to arrive, Cindy?" I raised my voice to make sure she could hear me.

"Well, Amanda was hoping you'd have time to do a quick fitting for the gowns she pulled for you, so the earlier the better," Cindy suggested.

Gowns? Plural?

I swallowed another sigh, not wanting Cindy to hear the disappointment in my voice because really it was my own fault for insisting on being an aspiring hermit. "We'll be there as early as we can." I grimaced, not wanting to provide an exact time in case I needed an extra hour in the shower to work through a complete mental breakdown in the morning.

"Wonderful." Cindy's approval was palpable, only offering a slight balm to my malaise. "Just bring yourselves—we'll have everything else you need."

"Okay, I guess we'll see you tomorrow. Bye, Mom." Chance winced.

"Bye, honey."

Shoulders tense, Chance ended the call and looked at me with dread.

"I'm not going to murder you in your sleep, if that's what you're thinking." I flopped back onto the bed in dramatic fashion. "I just need a minute to silently scream."

"Would another orgasm help?" he asked with chagrin.

"Probably," I huffed, earning a bark of laughter from Chance.

SATURDAY, DECEMBER 18

CHAPTER 3

"**S**weetheart, you need to wake up," Chance cooed, placing a soft kiss at my temple.

"Go away," I grumbled, turning over in bed.

I felt something move in front of my face and then the glorious aroma of a fresh latte hit my nose. My eyes sprung open and were met with a giant paper cup from my favorite local cafe.

I raised my gaze to meet Chance's blue-grey eyes, a smile curling my lips. "Thank you, baby," I purred, greedily taking the coffee from him and moaning as the first taste hit my tongue.

Chance leaned in, tucking a strand of hair behind my ear as I continued to take small sips of the steaming latte. "I packed all your things, but we should get on the road so we don't hit any traffic."

My posture deflated and my lips turned down, recalling the conversation with his mom the night before.

In an attempt to circumvent my incoming carping, Chance continued, "I confirmed with Amanda she has outfits ready for you for all of the events, even the more casual ones. She told me to just pack any toiletries or necessities. She also said we should have some downtime during the day while the events are being set up, so I've got a whole sack of books already packed in the car."

"What if I don't want to wear what she picked?" I groused, just trying to delay the inevitable.

Chance cupped my cheek in his palm. "You'll survive."

I gave him an exaggerated scowl in response, resulting in a howl of laughter from him. "C'mon." He took the coffee cup from me, set it on the nightstand, and reached for me to pull me out of bed.

While I'd never outright admit it to Chance, and let's be real, he probably knew anyway, I loved it when he fussed over me. Even better, I loved fussing over him later, to make sure he knew how much I appreciated him taking care of me.

Chance waited patiently in the living room while I got ready. Knowing I'd be giving up full control of my wardrobe for the next week, I slipped on my most comfortable pair of workout leggings, which also happened to be Chance's favorite pair of my workout leggings, and threw on one of his giant hoodies, reveling in the way it smelled so distinctly of him and his soap, wrapping me in warmth and comfort.

"Now you're just trying to make us late," Chance groaned, pulling me onto the couch to straddle him when I walked out to tell him I was ready to go and to harass him about where my coffee had gone. His hands encircled me, squeezing my ass as he bucked up into me.

"You're the one that wanted to leave so early," I murmured against his lips.

"You're going to make me suffer the entire three-hour drive, aren't you?" He wound his fingers through the hair at the base of my neck, tugging lightly.

I merely nodded, my smile wide.

"Let's get this over with then." He leaned forward, brushing his lips against mine tenderly.

After finishing my coffee, I pulled out my phone to go back over the full week's worth of events that would comprise what Cindy had dubbed the Harper House Winter Revelry.

I hadn't realized the first time I'd visited Chance's family estate that it actually had been passed down through his mother's family. While Thomas Roberts, Chance's father, also a billionaire business mogul and politician, came from plenty of money in his own right, Cindy's family was the kind of old-school wealth new money could only aspire to be, or so Amanda had told me over drinks during one of Chance's photography exhibitions.

I had no doubt the events we'd be attending would be filled with the who's who of New England society...just my luck. Thankfully, Chance had offered to talk through each of the events with me so I was as prepared as possible and at least had an understanding of what I could expect.

"Afternoon tea tomorrow is probably going to be the worst part, and you'll get it over with first," Chance offered.

"You're sure you can't come?" I pouted.

Chance glanced at me. "No boys allowed, I'm afraid. But Amanda will keep you company. She's always hated the more female-centric society events and will love to have a partner to gossip with in a corner all afternoon."

I smiled at that thought. Amanda, Chance's younger sister, had grown up in the society scene and still assisted their mother with events, but by day she was actually a programmer and designer, specializing in UX/UI development, which was how she'd met her partner, Hiram, an entrepreneur she'd worked with at a start-up.

It made me happy that we'd become closer over the past year. Sometimes when she was at events that Hiram wasn't able to attend, she'd live text me about all the drama going on. I never knew who any of the people were, but her commentary was enjoyable nonetheless.

"The fundraiser and charity auctions will be boring, but the food is usually decent. Mom will probably ask us to bid on something, so you can help me pick." He grinned at me.

"What kind of stuff do they have up for auction?" I was picturing material goods like on those auctioneering shows that used to be popular.

"Some of it's wild," Chance told me. "This is the kind of crowd that has access to a lot, but also the people who are donating want to kind of show off what they have, so plenty of vacations at insane locations, one-of-a-kind items, private tours or meetings with celebrities, that kind of stuff."

I felt my heart sinking at the thought of the type of wealth I'd be surrounded by. It was kind of my living nightmare. I was so far removed from the lives that those people led, I couldn't even imagine what they had access to. Hell, I couldn't even imagine a life where I didn't have to work for a living.

The fact that Chance came from such a high station felt unreal. Because the man I'd fallen in love with was so down-to-earth; he never made me feel less than. Tendrils of my anxiety began to writhe around inside. When it physically manifested in me starting to pick at my cuticles, Chance immediately noticed and grabbed my hand across the console.

I glanced up at him.

"You remember what we say, if all else fails?"

"Fuck 'em," I said quietly, repeating an inside joke we'd had from my first visit to his family's estate.

"It's going to be okay," he said softly, rubbing his thumb gently against my palm.

I nodded silently, afraid if I spoke again that my voice would crack or I'd spill my guts and he'd know the depths of my insecurities...He probably already knew...

"There is a reason I chose to leave this world behind," he stated. "These people do not have to struggle the way most do, so instead they create problems, whether it's with each other or by focusing on things so tiny and mundane it would amaze you, but they find a way."

I swallowed the lump in my throat.

"They will make you feel inadequate. They will infuriate you. They will trigger you," he warned. "But it's only because you have something they do not and something they can never hope to at-tain."

My brow furrowed in question.

"You have your integrity," he relayed. "But perhaps what they covet more is that while you struggle, you likely won't have to won-der if every single interaction you have with someone you're meeting for the first time, or those closest to you, has an ulterior motive.

"And I don't say this to make you pity them—they don't deserve it, but you must understand their disregard for anyone other than themselves is a result of their own issues, and not a testament of your true value."

I released a deep exhale at the thought.

"Many of the people you will meet this week are so deeply in-secure that anything you're working through yourself will pale in comparison to their own self-hatred. Because most of them haven't lived a single day of their life knowing for a fact that they are loved or wanted for who they are, instead of for their power or money. All the money in the world couldn't buy how deeply I care for you. And they all know that. They can never have what we have, and they will vilify you for it."

Chance squeezed my hand tightly. "And, Violet, you are very loved for *exactly* who you are."

I felt my lower lip trembling, the wave of emotion at his senti-ments overwhelming me. "I don't know what I'd do without you." I squeezed his hand back, blinking away tears.

He gave me a brilliant smile. "You won't have to find out—I'm keeping you."

I could only reply with a soft smile, appreciating him trying to lighten the mood.

"Tell me about the children's day." I needed to switch back to the event, or I'd become a ball of tears, and I didn't want to show up to his parents' house with a puffy red face and have them thinking we had been fighting on the drive over.

"When Mom's thrown similar events in the past, she's gone all out." Chance's eyes lit up. "She buses in disadvantaged kids from all over the state through all the children's charities she works with. It'll be loud, but it's a lot of fun."

I smiled at the thought of the mansion being overrun with children. "Will Santa be there?"

Chance glanced at me over his shoulder. "Why? Something you plan on asking for? I figured most of the things you wanted wouldn't be appropriate to share." His expression turned wicked.

"Well, you won't entertain the idea of us getting a dog, so I figured if I asked Santa, he might put in a good word for me." I laughed. Getting a pet had been a point of discussion for a while.

Chance wasn't exactly opposed, but he'd never had a pet growing up and he worried about whether or not we'd have the time needed to train a puppy, even though I told him I didn't want a puppy, I wanted a dog from the shelter. We hadn't come to an agreement, but it hadn't stopped me from looking and wanting and researching.

"Great," he grumbled. "You're going to turn Santa on me?"

"I might try," I teased.

"As for the other events, I know Amanda's excited for you to see your dress for the masquerade ball. She refused to give me even the smallest hint, so it must be amazing," Chance pondered.

The thought of Amanda being so thrilled about the gown was both exhilarating and terrifying. And when would I ever have the opportunity to go to a masquerade ball again?

"We'll have to suffer through the exclusive donor dinner on Christmas Eve, but I could always fake food poisoning," he joked.

My heart ached a little at the thought of being stuck at a dinner surrounded by stiff blue bloods on Christmas Eve, instead of tucked away and cozy in Chance's arms in our apartment. But there was always next year, I supposed.

"What else can I do to make this week easier for you?"

"Don't leave my side," I counted off on my fingers. "Don't allow your dad in my vicinity. Orgasms on demand—"

"You already have that," Chance laughed.

"And we reopen negotiations on getting a dog." I glared at him.

"We'll see."

I clicked my tongue at his non-committal response.

"If anyone says anything to you that you don't like, or bothers you, you come tell me immediately." Chance's demeanor had shifted to a more serious one. "I mean it." He squeezed my hand again. "I won't tolerate anyone disrespecting you."

I could have melted.

"Thank you."

"You can thank me when this nightmare of a week is over." He sighed.

"Deal."

CHAPTER 4

"I hope you like velvet and jewel tones!" Amanda greeted me with her patented sing-song voice, as well as a tight hug.

"Yipee," I deadpanned, earning a round of giggles from Chance's sister.

It had been a few months since I'd last seen her, but her naturally blonde hair was styled in long waves, complementing her tall, lean figure. She could have been a model if she'd wanted, but it made me love her more that she'd followed a passion that wasn't exactly common for women in her situation.

She'd once told me that she'd always been ostracized by certain women in her circles because of how seriously she took her studies and because she insisted on and enjoyed working full-time, even if she didn't have to. "Jealous little girls," she had snorted.

It was unfair that she was that stunning and even more intelligent. Some people have all the luck. But I loved her just the same.

We'd arrived at the house in time for a quick lunch and pleasantries with Amanda and Chance's mom, Cindy. Thankfully, his father was sequestered away on business in his study. Cindy looked like a slightly shorter version of her daughter, with the same color hair, although she kept hers trimmed to her shoulders, but still perfectly blown out. Both of Cindy's children had inherited her warm smile and charitable disposition.

And the house, good lord, it looked like Martha Stewart and a gaggle of elves had made their way through the entirety of the palatial, yet historical, mansion. Every banister was wrapped in garlands, each room had at least one Christmas tree—all with different, yet somehow corresponding themes—and brilliant red poinsettias were dotted around every room in tasteful arrangements. I felt like I was walking onto a holiday movie set.

It still didn't quite compute that a home like this was where Chance had spent a lot of his childhood. The house felt like it should be a museum—and I supposed it was about to turn into one—but a home for a small family...no, that didn't feel right. It was simply too large, too open, too cold, even with all the holiday decorations.

It lacked the crafty hominess of Christmas in a small family home. The decor was beautiful, but it was too well-groomed, too expertly arranged, too perfectly planned. My heart lurched at the memory of the popcorn garlands I'd made with my mom every year—the only decorations we could afford for the tree, other than paper ornaments I'd made in school, and a few that had been passed down in her family. It was quaint and rustic, but it was ours.

But this grand home, with holiday aesthetics to die for, lacked authenticity. It made me understand Chance that much more to have a better sense of how the holidays had felt for him. From the outside they looked like a dream, but inside, it had been lonely for him.

I was sure that Cindy had a team of decorators that had helped her make this cheerful vision come to life. Having gotten closer to both Cindy and Amanda over the last year, I knew how particular Cindy was about her space and decor, and Amanda...well, fashion was her obsession, and she made no qualms about letting me know she intended to play dress-up with me for the entirety of the week.

Just my luck.

After ogling the spacious entrance hall for a moment, much to Cindy's delight, Amanda eventually dragged me upstairs to Chance's bedroom to walk me through the wardrobe she'd curated for me for the week.

A tailor appeared out of nowhere to help with the gown fitting, while Chance and Hiram caught up in the seating area on one side of Chance's bedroom suite.

I hadn't interacted with Hiram much, but he seemed quite warm, albeit quiet. In a way, he was a perfect complement to Amanda's supermodel looks and easy charm. He was taller than her, wore glasses that made him look nerdy, but rather distinguished, and exuded a quiet confidence, which allowed her to take center stage. In fact he seemed to preen while watching her gregarious tendencies around others, as if her outgoing nature was one of his favorite qualities of hers.

Amanda had immediately been welcoming to me when I'd first met her the year before. Knowing she had a partner who appreciated her kindness warmed my little black heart.

After trying on each outfit, Amanda would parade me out into the bedroom and ask Chance for his thoughts. And for each outfit, he would shrug in indifference, amused by Amanda's anger at his lack of reaction.

But the second her back was turned, his eyes would turn sultry as they met my gaze, silently communicating a promise of what he wanted to do to me after getting to take each garment off the next time I'd wear them.

The only thing I wasn't able to try on was the gown for the masquerade ball. "The designer is putting on the finishing touches, but Jillian will confirm your measurements." Amanda nodded toward the seamstress, who had a mouth full of pins as she dutifully placed them along the hemline of my charity auction gown.

Due to Chance's antics, I was practically a puddle by the end of the session, and we were about to be late for what was sure to be an awkward dinner with his family when Amanda put me in a tight-fitting burgundy cashmere sweater and matching herringbone pencil skirt, complete with heels.

"Heels?" I complained.

"You'll be sitting all evening," Amanda snipped.

I huffed in distress. They were already pinching my toes.

"They look good." Chance came up next to me, sliding an arm around my waist.

Amanda glared at him. "Really? Now you comment on the clothes?"

Chance shrugged.

Amanda rolled her eyes.

I smiled, amused by their sibling antics.

"Let's go." Amanda laced her fingers through Hiram's and pulled him out of the room, calling out, "See you downstairs," as she left, closing the door behind her.

"You never wear skirts," Chance whispered, a dangerous edge to his voice as he ran the tip of his nose along the column of my neck, pressing himself against me from behind, making sure I was painfully aware of how hard he was.

"I didn't know you felt so strongly about them," I giggled, allowing Chance to push me forward until he had me sandwiched between him and his dresser.

"Neither did I, until I saw you in this one," he growled, placing his hand at the base of my neck and gently pushing me to bend forward, over the edge of the dresser, stopping only when my cheek hit the cold wood surface, my hands splayed in front of me.

"We're expected downstairs," I rasped, my breath hitching when I felt his fingers begin to pull the hem of the skirt up along my thighs and eventually over my ass.

I shivered, feeling the cooler air of the room hit my bare skin.

"Would you be mad if I asked you to wear heels more often?" His hands moved to the top of my panties, dragging them down my thighs at an infuriatingly slow pace.

"Depends. What do I get out of it?" I sassed.

I yelped when a sharp slap reverberated over one ass cheek, the pain quickly receding as his hand covered the sore spot by rubbing it with his warm palm. "You and I both know there isn't anything I wouldn't give you."

I smiled, sinking even further against the top of the dresser as he spread my bare cheeks apart, his cock rubbing through the wetness gathered at my core a moment later.

"We'll be late..." The words turned into a moan as he slid inside me.

"Let them wait," he snarled, continuing to slowly push until he was all the way in.

"This won't be gentle," Chance warned.

"Good." I smiled, pushing back against him, loving how full I felt with him inside me.

Chapter 5

When we entered the spacious dining room, which smelled of cedar and wine, due to the heavy and likely genuine garland that was draped around the perimeter of the room, twenty minutes late, every single head snapped to us. I was sure my cheeks were blazing. I smoothed my hair nervously, praying that nobody could tell how freshly fucked I was, or the fact that I wasn't wearing any panties because Chance had refused to return them to me after he'd railed me against his dresser—the scoundrel.

To my relief, a moment later they returned to their conversation, while picking at salads, and Chance and I took our places across from Amanda and Hiram. I noticed Chance bristled at having to sit next to his father, but with his parents at the head of either side of the table, it was inevitable that one of us would have to sit next to him, and I appreciated that Chance took the bullet in my stead.

Thankfully, most of the dinner conversation was about the upcoming events, although I felt Thomas's assessing gaze lingering on me out of the corner of my eye multiple times. I couldn't help but harbor a grudge against the man, not just for how long he'd denied helping Daniel, but also because of how he'd treated Chance while growing up.

Instead of nurturing a creative and sensitive boy, he'd treated him as less than, constantly compared him to others, and alienated him. So while I could be polite to Thomas Roberts, I would remain distant. I didn't think I was capable of forgiving him for the trauma he'd inflicted upon his son.

And what was ironic was that Chance was still a product of his father, but perhaps in ways that Thomas might not have recognized. His success was often touted as a result of his analytical skills and good judgment of character, traits that both his children possessed in spades, but utilized differently.

Where Thomas used them to get ahead in business, Amanda wielded her abilities to forge genuine connections and friendships in a sea of imposters, and similarly, Chance not only used those skills to do the same, but also to take it one step farther and to observe those he cared about to be the best partner, friend, sibling, or son, he could be, tailored to their needs and expectations.

I supposed that was where Cindy's influence had shaped her children, pivoting them toward selflessness as they'd grown up watching her use her wealth and power to give back to the community, rather than to grow an empire. Still, she supported Thomas in his efforts, so nobody was perfect.

However, over dessert, the veneer of this perfect family managed to fracture just enough for me to see through the facade.

"I have an announcement to make," Amanda stated; all eyes went to her. "Hiram and I are going to be moving to California at the end of January."

Cindy dropped her dessert fork with a clatter.

"No, you're not," Thomas scoffed.

Amanda's jaw clenched in anger, and I noticed Hiram's arm move as he looked to have grabbed her hand under the table, a silent sign of his support.

Next to me, Chance leaned back, ready to take in the show, it appeared. Me, on the other hand—I was frozen like a deer in the headlights, not wanting to be caught in any sort of private family affairs.

"Hiram's business has taken off and he needs to be based out of the Bay to keep an eye on things," Amanda continued, her voice tight.

"Why didn't you tell me sooner?" Cindy's voice wavered.

Amanda's face fell. "It all kind of happened so fast—we thought it would take a lot longer to find a house, and you were so busy with the event planning..."

"You're not going," Thomas repeated.

Amanda glared at him. "Daddy, with all due respect, I'm an adult. You can't stop me."

"No, but I could cut you off," he stated coldly, setting his napkin down on his plate.

Unfortunately for me, I wasn't able to stifle a short, but appalled, gasp at his threat, earning the attention of everyone at the table for a brief moment. Chance's hand squeezed my knee under the table to comfort me.

"Don't listen to him," Cindy cut in, waving a hand at Thomas to dismiss the intimidation tactic.

"And what do you have to say for yourself, young man?" Thomas turned his attack on Hiram, who, to his credit, remained calm under Thomas's scrutiny. "If you have plans of proposing, you won't have my blessing."

"Thomas, stop," Cindy said more forcefully, cutting him off from doing more damage. She reached across the table to grab Amanda's hand. "We'll always support you. Will you come back to visit?"

"Of course," Amanda said resolutely. "And you can come see me too. You'll love the house, and you know I'll want your help decorating."

The tension in Cindy's shoulders lessened as she smiled softly at her daughter. "I'd love that."

Having had enough, Thomas swiftly stood from his chair and strode out of the room without looking back.

"Don't worry about him—he'll come around. He's just overprotective," Cindy reassured Amanda, patting her hand.

"I really didn't mean to keep it from you."

"I know, honey." Cindy gave Amanda a watery smile. "And I'll talk to him." She turned to Hiram. "He just needs a minute to process everything."

Hiram nodded, but I could sense he knew there were still battles to be fought.

With the dinner having come to an unceremonious conclusion, Chance and I were heading out to retire to our room for the evening when he stopped me. "I need to talk to my mom for a minute. I'll be up in a bit."

I nodded, curious, but thinking perhaps he wanted to console her or let her know that he and I had no plans of leaving anytime soon, to ease her heartache. Unfortunately, my exhaustion from having to get up so early, as well as the anticipatory stress for the events that would kick off the next day, caught up with me. I fell asleep before Chance returned.

SUNDAY,
DECEMBER 19

CHAPTER 6

"You have to go with a pinky-nude." Amanda grabbed my hand to hold different nail polish shades against my skin tone. "It's neutral, so it will match all your outfits, no matter what you wear."

"But you picked a bright red." I used my free hand to point to the bottle of polish that was sitting on the table next to her.

"Yes, well, that's a neutral for me." Amanda grinned.

Cindy laughed in agreement on my other side.

Despite it having not been on the schedule of events, I was dragged out of bed at an obscene hour for what Amanda was calling a spa morning before our dreadful afternoon tea with all the high society ladies.

Thankfully, Chance must have enlightened Amanda about my requirement for coffee to function, so while I feasted on pastries and lattes, Cindy and Amanda ran through all the various beauty treatments they had booked for the three of us before the event.

I wasn't exactly comfortable with all of the services, as I'd never been able to afford to do any of them before, but I appreciated so much that I had been included in such an intimate activity that

Amanda and Cindy could have easily excluded me from, designating it a mother-daughter affair.

But what I enjoyed a bit more than us taking turns getting manicures, pedicures, massages, and the like was listening to the two of them talk about the women who would be attending the tea party later.

"I need to see the seating chart before the event," Amanda told her mom. "I need to make sure Lydia Whitmore isn't anywhere near Violet and me." She turned to me to provide more context. "She makes women cry at charity luncheons for sport."

My mouth gaped at the thought.

"I have you next to Juliette Hargrove and her sister," Cindy replied.

Amanda rolled her eyes. "How did she manage to get on the list?"

"Called in a favor." Cindy shrugged.

Again, Amanda turned to me conspiratorially. "The Hargroves are new money social climbers, so she'll be nice, but don't give her an inch—she'll take a mile and then start using your name to score more invites."

"Joke's on her." I snorted. "Nobody knows who I am."

Amanda cocked her head. "Is that what you think?"

I tensed at the implication. "Why would they?"

"You're the elusive French heiress my brother ran off with after last year's New Year's Eve gala, don't you remember?" Amanda shoved me as she giggled. "Nobody else has forgotten."

"Imagine what they'll think when they find out I'm a lowly school teacher without a penny to my name?" I gave a sardonic snort. "I barely get an invite to faculty mixers at Montgomery."

Amanda frowned. "Teaching is a respectable profession," she stated. "And Chance said the other teachers are all scared of you, which is why they were hesitant to invite you."

That earned a howl of laughter from me. "Oh yeah?" I chuckled. "What else did Chance say?"

Amanda's smile softened. "He also complains to me all the time about how you insist on splitting bills and won't let him help you out with anything."

Cindy pretended she was focused on her nails being painted, but I knew she had overheard.

Now it was my turn to frown. "He shouldn't have told you that," I said in a hushed whisper.

Amanda shook her head. "He just wants to make things easier for you. He sees you struggling and it tears him up inside when he could take all of it away."

I swallowed the lump in my throat. This was perhaps the only disagreement that Chance and I hadn't been able to work through yet. "I refuse to take anything from him," I admitted.

"Why?" Amanda didn't understand.

"Because it would change things between us, no matter how small the amount, whether or not I paid it back," I confessed, having made that mistake before and learning the hard way what happened when I relied on someone else, even temporarily, while I got on my feet. Nothing came without a cost. "I would rather struggle until my loans are paid off and my mom's mortgage is taken care of than have Chance worry for a moment that I wasn't with him for the right reasons."

She released a deep exhale, hopefully understanding my position. Amanda reached out and squeezed my hand. "I'm sorry."

"We'll figure it out," I replied, wanting to talk about anything else at that moment.

Thankfully, Amanda seemed to have the same thought and continued with her assessment of the rest of our tablemates.

While Cindy, ever the diplomat, always tried to see the best in people, Amanda was much more shrewd with her commentary, although it sounded like the women that had earned Amanda's ire deserved it, as her notes weren't petty, but rather focused on the lack of character and questionable actions of the other society ladies.

"What's on your Christmas list this year, dear?" Cindy asked me softly, while Amanda was sequestered next door during her turn with the masseuse.

"Well, I want a dog, but your son is being stubborn about it," I joked.

A thoughtful expression crossed Cindy's face. "He always wanted one growing up, but we traveled so often, it just didn't make sense. I knew the staff would end up doing most of the work, and they were busy enough as it was, so we just never got one."

Chance hadn't told me that. I wondered what had changed.

"Do you know what he wants? Or have you already gotten him something?" she hedged.

I squirmed a little, earning a quick tut from the nail technician working on my pedicure. "Chance and I agreed we weren't going to do gifts this year," I divulged.

Cindy said nothing, but cocked her head as she digested the information.

Wanting to fill the uncomfortable silence, I continued, "We just spent all this money moving into the apartment over the summer, and neither of us are big gift people...one less thing for us to worry about, I suppose..."

"That's alright," she offered in a comforting tone. "I was just hoping you might have some ideas for me. He doesn't call me as much since he's so busy with school."

"Oh." I gulped. "Well, if you wanted an idea for yourself—he normally prefers using the antique cameras he's collected over the years for his photography." I laughed inwardly, thinking about how Chance had immediately commandeered the laundry room as a dark room and moved the washer and dryer out to the garage when we'd first moved in. "But he's mentioned that he might be interested in getting a DSLR camera to start shooting some stuff in digital."

Her eyes brightened. "Is there one in particular he has his eye on?"

She knew her son well. "I'll send you the link." I smiled.

"Wonderful." Cindy beamed. She opened her mouth to say something, but then closed it a moment later. I wondered if maybe she wanted to ask the same of me, but thought better of it. I wouldn't even give Chance any ideas other than nagging him about a dog, which at this point was becoming more of a schtick than anything, as his hesitancy made me reluctant to follow through.

"I'm glad you could make it this week." Cindy gave me another kind smile. "It means a lot to me."

"Thank you for including me," I told her honestly.

"Of course," she said simply. "You're family, dear."

Those words and the ease with which she said them softened me more than I'd expected.

CHAPTER 7

The tea party dress Amanda had chosen for me felt more appropriate for spring than the middle of winter, but there were small touches that had been added to the design to denote the season in which it would be worn.

The solid lining of the dress was a dusty rose color made of the softest silk I'd ever felt against my body, but where the real artistry lay was in the matching, translucent chiffon overlay, which sported an array of small winter florals and snowflakes embroidered along the fabric. The snowflakes were stitched with thread that had metallic pieces, so when they caught the light, the dress glimmered ever so slightly.

It had a modest V-neck, was tapered at the waist with a satin ribbon at my waistline, and tied with a bow at the back. The dress was the perfect tea length on me, hitting at mid-calf. Unfortunately, I would have to suffer through the afternoon in nude pumps that complemented the garment well, but the dress itself fit like a dream and was surprisingly comfortable. The sparkling diamond solitaire necklace Chance had gifted me at the New Year's gala the year before was also flawless, paired with the pearl clip Amanda had fastened to pull back one side of my hair.

As someone who defaulted to wearing black mostly because it hid stains and wear best and allowed me to easily slink into the background, I'd never felt more feminine in my life...almost like a different version of myself.

"Remember, don't let anything these women say get to you," Amanda reminded me as we made our way down the stairs. "They're a bunch of jealous harpies who have nothing better to do than be cruel to other women."

I nodded, holding tight to the railing so I wouldn't slip on my heels and break my neck, or worse, make a spectacle of myself in front of the society ladies gathered in the entrance hall. I focused on taking one step at a time, instead of on the attention I knew Amanda and I would be receiving as we descended into the fray.

Beyond the grand entrance hall, where women tittered and nibbled on passed hors d'oeuvres, the ballroom was filled with tables clad in deep burgundy fabric. The Christmas trees around the room had been redecorated overnight to reflect the color palette of the tea party, including the burgundy, as well as a blush pink and pearlescent ivory. The feminine holiday tones felt more than appropriate for the gathering, and once again I found myself in awe of my surroundings.

A waiter approached, offering us both glasses of champagne as I took in the scene and Amanda scanned the various attendees, deciding in which order she wanted to greet them. I was pleased to see that, while there appeared to be tea available on the tables, it seemed most women held a stemmed glass filled with some sort of alcoholic beverage in their dainty hands.

I followed Amanda around dutifully while she made her rounds, giving air kisses and pleasantries to those she liked and stilted smiles and quick greetings to those she didn't.

But after trailing her for a while, and with the programming still a half hour away from beginning, my feet were killing me. "Can I go sit down?" I whispered as she wrapped up her conversation with an older woman she had happily chatted with.

Amanda gave me a quick frown. "I need to keep saying hello to everyone—technically, I'm co-hosting with Mom."

I supposed that meant she had to greet everyone who was in attendance to be polite, lest she be cast out of society for failing to be a proper hostess.

I glanced down at my feet. "I'll be okay if I just sit at our table for a minute."

She seemed to contemplate it for a moment. "If you're sure you'll be alright on your own."

I nodded, thinking that unpleasant small talk would be worth getting off my feet.

"We're at table four." She motioned toward the head of the room. "I'll try to finish up quickly."

"Thank you." I smiled, giving her arm a quick squeeze before slipping through the crowd and taking a seat at my designated place.

It took less than a minute for someone to come sit down next to me.

"Terribly drab event, don't you think?" an elegant voice said from beside me.

I looked over to find a stunning young woman with long, wavy red hair, brilliant blue eyes, and the kind of natural beauty one could only dream of. To make matters worse, she wore an eggplant-colored, off-the-shoulder dress that further accentuated every curve and piece of exposed skin.

"The house is beautiful, at least, but these tea parties usually dissolve into self-congratulatory speeches over charity works," the woman told me, clearly understanding that I was out of place and didn't know how things usually went.

I merely hummed in neither agreement nor disagreement, not knowing how to respond and unsure if her comments were meant to connect with me or to undermine Cindy's hard work, somehow.

"Simone Charles." She put her hand out to shake, which I reciprocated, holding back a wince when her hand dropped into mine so featherlight and limp, I wasn't sure how I was supposed to shake it. Was this the way society women were taught to shake hands? Did it communicate how delicate and unthreatening they were to potential suitors?

"Violet Price," I offered my name as I retracted my hand, before immediately downing the rest of my champagne.

"I haven't seen you at one of these before," she called me out, but I still couldn't tell what her motives were. Was she friend or foe?

"This is my first," I confirmed her suspicions.

"I love your dress. I think I wore it in a different colorway a few seasons ago." She smiled, flagging a nearby waiter and grabbing a glass of red wine from his tray, while I was able to snatch another glass of champagne for myself.

Foe, then.

"Yes, I borrowed it from Amanda." What Simone didn't realize was that I couldn't have cared less how old my clothes were, how much they cost, whether they were trendy, or if I had borrowed them from someone else.

Her eyebrows raised at the implication. "You're Chance's girl…" She trailed off, brows furrowing at the realization and her gaze becoming much more assessing than before.

I gave her a tight smile. "I am." The word "girl" seemed reductive, especially since I estimated that Simone and I were roughly the same age.

She leaned back in her chair. "You're the talk of the town, you know."

I clenched my jaw; that was the last thing I needed to hear. "Oh, really?"

Then Simone leaned forward again. "There's a pool amongst the women on how long you'll last before he gets tired of slumming it."

Amanda had warned me. I knew what I was walking into. I thought I was prepared. I thought I could handle these women.

I was wrong.

"Where'd you place your bets?" I tried my best to seem unaffected, taking a sip from my glass.

"Not too much longer." She tapped her perfectly manicured nails against the table. "He'll wait until after the holidays to break things off—needs someone on his arm for events so he isn't overwhelmed with interest or pressured to find a new date. And he's not cruel, so he wouldn't do it during the season, you know..."

"I see," I seethed.

"Most people are already out. They didn't think you'd last over a month, let alone a year." She lowered her voice. "So what's your secret? Freaky shit in the bedroom? Guilt-tripping him because you're destitute?"

I snorted a laugh.

"Seriously, why would he want someone like you when he could have his pick of any eligible woman in this room? You're...*nothing*." She scoffed.

I took a deep breath, steeling myself as I tried to decide how I wanted to play this. Should I ignore her? She already knew she'd hit her mark. I could play into her hand, telling her what she wanted to hear, but I didn't want to debase myself like that. However, if I fought back, it could cause a scene, and I couldn't have that. I was stuck.

"Well?" she snapped.

"I see you've met my soon-to-be sister-in-law." Amanda's voice came from behind me, saving me from having to make a decision.

Simone's eyes flashed up to Amanda, shocked by her declaration. And I should have been as well, but I knew she was just trying to help, even if it was a lie.

"I was just introducing myself to Violet." She stood so she was at Amanda's level.

"She doesn't need to be introduced to you." Amanda's voice was polite, but there was heat beneath her words.

"It was nice to meet you, Violet." Simone glared down at me, grabbing for her wineglass to leave.

"The pleasure was all mine," I sneered.

As if in slow motion, I watched the expression morph on Simone's face at the same time that she tipped her wineglass, emptying the contents of the red liquid into my lap.

"Oh dear, I'm so sorry," she feigned.

Amanda went rigid for a moment. If looks could kill, Simone would have died on the spot. But ever the professional, she pushed past Simone, who had already turned to leave, giggling as she went, to get help from a waiter to help sop up the wine.

"I'm sorry I ruined your dress," I whispered to Amanda, blinking back tears, as she sat down to help me dab a fabric napkin at the stain, a useless effort.

"You didn't—she did." Amanda accepted a stack of folded napkins from a waiter who brought them over. "I shouldn't have left you."

I didn't reply.

"Simone briefly dated Chance in high school," Amanda told me. "She's been trying to get him back ever since he broke up with her, after he found out she and her friends had bullied me."

I swallowed the lump in my throat, still hearing her voice ringing in my ears. *You're...nothing.*

"The dress is replaceable," Amanda told me, catching my gaze. "*You* are not."

"I need to change." I stood from the chair, relieved to see the stain hadn't managed to seep through to the cushion.

"I can go with you," Amanda offered, her eyes troubled.

I shook my head. "You need to attend to things around here." I didn't want her inconvenienced any further because I couldn't manage to be on my own for two minutes without making an enemy.

"Okay," she sighed, clearly unhappy about it, but she couldn't disagree that her presence would be missed. "There are a couple of backup options on the rack—any of them will work."

"Thank you." I took the napkins from her, holding them to the dress, trying to hide the stain, although I could feel the attention from everyone in the room on me already.

Amanda's hand snagged on my wrist. "Please come back," she whispered.

I said nothing, not wanting to make a promise I couldn't keep.

I bowed my head, refusing to make eye contact with anyone as I skirted around the perimeter of the room, but instead of taking the stairs up to Chance's room, I found myself being drawn to the back hallway...to the atrium, where I'd realized last year that I had fallen in love with Chance.

CHAPTER 8

The atrium looked so different in the bright daylight than it had in the dark of night when I'd last been there with Chance. And although the twinkling fairy lights weren't on, the room was no less magical.

The semicircular room had a bowed wall of glass, providing a spectacular view of the back lawn, where I watched workers bustling to build pieces for the children's festival that would happen later in the week.

I sulked in my soiled dress, plopping down on one of the benches, not wanting to risk getting a wine stain on any of the upholstered furniture dotting the room, in between large planters and flower beds.

The gentle trickle of a water feature in the corner gave me something to focus on, other than the utter humiliation I had just suffered at the hands of Chance's ex, in front of all the high society women in the tri-state area.

I knew I wouldn't be returning to tea, despite Amanda's plea. I didn't even want to have to go upstairs to face Chance and be forced to tell him what had happened, let alone return to a room full of hostile socialites masquerading as paragons of virtue.

How had I ever thought I could even attempt to fit in or at least go unnoticed amongst these women? This elite group would never accept me. Did that mean that my relationship with Chance was doomed to fail if these outside influences began to infiltrate our happiness?

We'd been living in a bubble in our quaint little rental house that I'd insisted we go with because I'd refused to allow Chance to pay more than half of the bills for a newer apartment. But that wasn't real life. Real life was the room full of whispering aristocrats that watched me be degraded and said nothing.

By committing to a life with Chance, I was opening myself up to their judgment and criticism, whether I wanted to or not, because my appearance and my actions reflected on him, and in turn, reflected on his family. I wasn't sure I'd ever be able to develop skin thick enough to weather the commentary that would follow us for the rest of our lives.

Nothing I did or said would ever be good enough for them...because I hadn't been born into their world.

As if hearing my spiraling from the depths of the house, a figure sat down next to me on the bench. The alluring and comforting aroma of Chance's fresh soap scent was unmistakable.

"You look beautiful in that dress," he said softly, twining his fingers through mine.

"Too bad it's ruined," I muttered.

He nodded quietly, acknowledging my embarrassment without dismissing it. "Amanda told me what happened."

I huffed out a sigh.

He squeezed my hand in response, giving me the space I needed to process things, while offering the physical comfort I had come to depend on from him.

"I didn't know you were into redheads." I glowered.

Chance chuckled. "I'm not." He leaned in against me, his warm breath caressing my ear when he whispered, "I've got a thing for sassy brunettes, and you know that." He placed a soft kiss just behind my ear, eliciting a shiver that tingled as it ran down my spine.

"Do you want to talk about what happened?" he asked quietly a moment later.

"No."

"Are you willing to listen?"

I nodded solemnly, my gaze trailing along the edge of a crack in one of the large granite tiles just below my foot.

"You fancy yourself a misanthrope and mistake me for someone who likes everyone," Chance began, "but just because I get along with most people doesn't mean I like them. In fact, I might dislike people more than even you."

I snorted a laugh at the thought. Chance was so gregarious, his charisma knew no bounds, which, on days like today, had me wondering what on earth someone like him saw in someone like me, who would rather be left to my own devices, albeit with one exception now, thanks to him.

"Can I tell you a secret?" His hushed tone held a note of conspiratorial merriment.

I nodded against him.

"I hate them all," he confessed.

I choked back a laugh.

"So many of the women in that room, and the men who will join them later this week, whether directly or indirectly, made my life miserable while I was growing up," Chance admitted.

My shoulders slumped upon hearing the pain in his words.

"I know how difficult it is to ignore them, or pretend the awful things they say and do don't hurt. They cut so deep, I thought I'd never be able to mend the wounds. But I have." He paused. "Do you know how?"

I looked up at him, getting lost in his blue-grey eyes for a moment before shaking my head in response.

"Because of people that have come into my life and been true friends, offering unconditional support, without the promise of receiving anything in return." He drew a deep breath, his lips hovering near my ear again when he said quietly, "People like you, Violet."

And it broke something in me, to think that he'd had to go so long without knowing what real love or friendship meant. I turned to him, burying my face in his chest and snaking my arms around his waist. He returned the gesture, pulling me even closer.

"If you insist on allowing other people's opinions to influence you, then at least let them be the opinions of those who love you," he advised. "I think you're brilliant and kind and gorgeous, and since the day I met you, not a moment has passed where you haven't been on my mind. I would hope that how I see you holds much more weight than what anyone in that room thinks."

I peered up at him, blinking back tears, wanting to allow his words to seep into me, but still fighting against them, despite my best efforts. "But what are you even getting out of this relationship?" I argued. "I don't bring anything to the table. All I do is complain."

In a surprising move, Chance burst into laughter.

I frowned in confusion at his response.

He brought his hand up, using his pointer finger to attempt to smooth out the creases in my brow. "You're so adorable."

"Don't patronize me." I grabbed his finger, pulling it down between us.

"You're my muse," he offered.

"Be serious."

He cocked his head, watching me for a moment. "I'm a dreamer, and without your guidance as a realist, I might never get my head out of the clouds. You're pragmatic and organized, where I am idealistic and abstract. You help me find the path I need to follow my dreams, and I'm trying to help you figure out how to dream. We fit like two perfect little maladapted puzzle pieces, don't you think?" He gave me a soft smile.

And I wanted to agree with him. I did agree with him. But what if love wasn't enough? What if *I* wasn't enough?

"I feel like I'm not good enough for you—for your world," I blurted out my thoughts against my will.

"Violet, *you* are my world." He stared down at me resolutely. As if that should be the most obvious thing in the world. And maybe it should have been.

How did this man manage to make me fall more deeply in love with him with every single day that passed?

"I love you," I whispered, just before leaning up to kiss Chance.

He sighed against my lips, opening his mouth to me, allowing me to explore him with slow and tender intent, returning each stroke in kind before gently pulling away and resting his forehead against mine.

"I love you too, sweetheart." He punctuated the sentiment with another short peck to my lips.

"You'll get sick of me eventually," I half-joked.

"Never," he rumbled, kissing me soundly once more, before releasing me. "Let's hole away upstairs and binge-watch something on TV. I can have the staff bring dinner to us, and if you're up for it later, the bathtub in my room can easily fit two people." He raised an eyebrow suggestively.

"Oh?" I asked. "And how would you know?"

He chuckled.

"Simone better not have been in that fucking bathtub before me," I growled.

Chance merely shook his head as he stood from the bench. "Nobody has been in that bathtub except for me, and seriously, I only dated her for a couple weeks over fifteen years ago."

He extended a hand to help me up. "But I have to admit, it's kind of hot when you're jealous."

"Fuck off." I scowled, grabbing his outstretched hand.

However, when I got to my feet, my heel caught on the cracked tile and I tipped backward, taking the bench with me as I fell, ass-first, into a pot with a giant tree in the middle of the room, wincing as the bench hit the floor with a harsh crack.

"Are you okay?" Chance rushed toward me, reaching out to help me to my feet.

"Yeah," I grumbled, ignoring the pain shooting up my tailbone. "I might be cursed, though." I prayed that stupid bench wasn't some sort of relic, or his parents would probably never forgive me.

Chance just shook his head at me and helped me dust off the dirt that now marred the back of the dress. Could this day get any worse?

I glanced down at the overturned bench. One spindly leg lay cattywampus, and there was a chunk broken off the underside, with something else pinned beneath it.

"What's that?" I pointed to the weathered, brown material.

Chance sank to his haunches and was able to pull it out. It appeared to be a very old leather portfolio.

"Open it," I encouraged him, leaning over his shoulder.

Following my direction, he unfastened the tie and revealed a stack of aged papers. Gingerly, he slipped them from the leather, fanning them out a bit, which showed two sets of handwriting on alternating pages, one a flourishing script, and the other a scrawl.

I held my hand out expectantly, and Chance passed me a few of the pages.

"Who's Mitzi?" I asked, noting the signature at the bottom of one of the pages with the more feminine cursive.

Chance glanced back up at me. "That's my grandmother." His gaze fell to the necklace resting at the base of my neck.

I scanned the page in front of me, able to pick out most of the writing, although the elegant script made some words harder than others. "My heart beats only to find its echo in yours," I read the beautiful words aloud.

"They're love letters," Chance breathed in awe.

MONDAY, DECEMBER 20

CHAPTER 9

"This one goes after the one you're holding." I swapped pages with Chance.

We'd spent all evening poring over the letters we'd discovered and were working to put them in order after an initial read-through. The bed was a mess with piles of half-organized stacks cluttering every inch, with Chance and I next to each other in the middle, trying to keep track of it all.

I remembered what Chance had told me about how his grandmother had been a bit of a live wire, causing all sorts of scandals, and after reading her often salacious letters, I could believe it; she was an absolute spitfire.

The letters we'd uncovered spanned just over two years, between 1938 and 1940. Chance estimated his grandmother would have been around sixteen when the letters began, up to eighteen when they ended. Although the latest dating letter we had in the pile didn't appear to be an end to the letters or the young lovers' affair, simply an end to the cache we had found.

I began to re-read the top of the stack. Now that we had them in chronological order, it would be much easier to understand their progression.

"There's references to them having exchanged notes for a long time, like since they were children, but at some point the friendship turned romantic when they were teenagers. It sounds like they were both pretty lonely and only had each other."

"She would have been alone here," Chance told me. "Grandma Mitzi always joked about being a surprise baby. Her sisters were quite a bit older than her and were already married with families of their own. That's probably why she ended up getting to keep the house."

And the boy in question was Sasha, the gardener's son. According to the letters, his family immigrated to the US during the Bolshevik Revolution, and he was actually born in Maine. He didn't seem to have any friends of his own, but the way the two of them talked in the letters, it seemed they had known each other their whole lives and carried on a secret friendship during their childhood.

The way they spoke to each other was so intimate and passionate it almost hurt to read. The pair seemed to be so in love, and the fact that they were separated by their social classes was heartbreaking.

Although Chance and I hadn't exactly faced the same adversity, there were pieces of the letters that reminded me of our story...one I was still trying to work through.

Mitzi seemed to struggle so much with the idea that external influence made it impossible for her to be with him. And Sasha loved her so much he was both willing to walk away if that made her happy, or content to live in the shadows of her life if it meant he could have even the smallest piece of her without causing her public disgrace.

My gut twisted at the thought that things between them surely had to have ended, because Chance's grandfather wasn't named Sasha, but Alexander, Chance's namesake. I was desperate to find out what happened to the two of them. I had so many questions.

Where was Sasha?

Where were the rest of the letters?

Why was this stack hidden in a compartment under the atrium bench?

"Do you know what she means here?" I pointed to the bottom of one of her letters.

"'I'll see you beneath the hummingbird,'" Chance read aloud.

"And that's not the only time it's mentioned." I paged through the letters and found a dozen references in them, from both Mitzi and Sasha, showing each of them to Chance.

"I'm not sure. It must have been where they met in secret," he guessed. His eyebrows shot up suddenly. "Wait, there was something else. Hold on." He paged through the stack in a rush, but still attempted to be gentle with the brittle paper. "I think they must have had a secret meeting place in the house somewhere—look."

Chance handed me one of the letters written by Mitzi and pointed out a specific paragraph.

Forgive me for missing our meeting yesterday. After that dreadful Mrs. Booker found the key beneath my mattress last week, I had no choice but to find a better hiding spot beyond my room. Unfortunately, time and unexpected company were not in my favor this evening, as the Darbys decided to pay a last-minute visit, keeping me from retrieving it and from you.

"Why would she need a key to meet him?" I questioned.

"It sounds like they were doing a lot more than talking when they were meeting up, and they weren't doing it in her room, so maybe they had a hidden place where they could spend time together without having to worry about being caught," Chance suggested.

"One that required a key only Mitzi would have access to," I added. "You think there's a secret room or passage around here?"

Chance shrugged. "It's an old mansion. It was built in the eighteen hundreds. I'd be surprised if there *weren't* some secret nooks and crannies."

We continued to read through the letters late into the night and early into the next morning, absorbing everything we could about Mitzi and Sasha, as well as searching for more clues about where they would meet and the key Mitzi had mentioned.

"Okay, there was definitely a secret room," Chance declared, dropping one of Sasha's letters in my lap. "Look at the last sentence."

I saw Booker sniffing around by the hummingbird while I was pruning the roses this morning. Be careful you aren't followed. If they discover our room, they will find us next.

My bleary eyes widened, meeting Chance's gaze. "Nice work!" I leaned over, giving him a peck on the cheek, earning a soft smile and a hint of a blush. "Where are there roses on the property?"

Chance sighed. "Everywhere. I'm not sure if it will narrow it down."

"They're everywhere now, but maybe there were less back then. Does your family keep any old photo albums we could look through?"

"In my dad's study." Chance cringed.

I bit my lip in thought and looked across to the clock on Chance's desk. "It's past two in the morning. Would he still be up?"

Chance shook his head. "No, but he keeps it locked."

"Oh..." *Drat.*

"If I find an opportunity tomorrow to sneak in, I'll take it. But I remember there being a lot of albums."

"We just need ones that are from the two years they were writing in these letters."

Chance nodded. "We'll find it."

"You think?" I set down the pages on the bed, suddenly exhausted. "It could be a needle in a haystack."

"The house hasn't changed much since I was growing up. Maybe some new paint and drapes. I bet there's a decent chance we could find the key and the room." Chance observed me thoughtfully. "And if anyone can find it, it's you." He gave me a tired smile.

"I just need to know what happened to them," I confessed quietly.

He placed a comforting hand on my thigh. "I know."

Perhaps it was just a lark to try chasing down ghosts in this mansion, but it meant the world to me that there wasn't a single moment where Chance questioned me, or wasn't firmly along for the ride. Just like always, he was at my side no matter what.

CHAPTER 10

"Stupid fucking hummingbirds," I muttered, while Amanda worked to zip me into my dress for the political fundraiser on Monday night.

"What?" Amanda stopped zipping. "Did I accidentally catch you in the zipper?"

"No, it's fine." I sighed.

Who would have thought there'd be a million hummingbirds all over the stupid fucking house? Not me.

After staying up until the crack of dawn going through the letters, Chance and I had slept in until almost lunch, to his mother's horror and his father's perturbed glaring, and then we'd spent the afternoon dodging around event staff to search for hummingbirds around the mansion, hoping they might give us a clue as to where the entrance to the secret meeting location was.

The problem wasn't just the infinite amount of hummingbirds scattered around the home inlaid in the wood, in the background of paintings, figurines of all different materials, and on multiple fabrics, but also the fact that neither Chance nor I had any idea of how we could identify the entrance to a secret room.

"What if there's like a hidden lever or something? How are we supposed to find that?" I'd complained to Chance during our ill-fated search. "There are a million books in your family's library—it would take us forever to test each one."

"You've been watching too much Scooby Doo, muse." Chance chuckled. His laughter doubled in volume when I scowled in response.

I'd known it was a long shot that we'd find anything, but I had to admit I'd gotten my hopes up. And reading the love story unfold between Mitzi and Sasha had touched something inside me. I knew I wouldn't let it go until I had found some sort of resolution.

"How does it feel? Can you breathe?" Amanda asked, stepping back after finishing all the fastenings of the dress.

I nodded, running my hands down the super soft, and thankfully stretchy, deep emerald velvet fabric. The floor-length dress had a low V-neck in the front and a scoop back that exposed the planes of my back, while still somehow managing to look modest, probably due to the long sleeves and elegant train that trailed behind me.

Amanda's hair stylist had fashioned my hair in a loose chignon, with wispy tendrils framing my face. As usual, Amanda had allowed me to do my own minimal makeup, which mostly consisted of mascara and a tinted gloss. I'd never worn a gown this elegant before, and I felt like a different person, in a good way—like I was the most refined version of myself.

A low whistle sounded from the doorway. Both Amanda and I turned our heads to regard Chance, with Hiram's taller frame peeking out around his shoulder.

God, Chance was gorgeous. Seeing him in a well-tailored tuxedo, not a hair out of place, made me want to melt. How on earth did this man belong to me? What was wrong with him that he didn't see he could get any woman he wanted, yet he had chosen me? None of it made sense.

"You look gorgeous," he simpered, placing a soft kiss at my temple before wrapping an arm around my waist, slowly moving it down to stroke the fabric at my hip. "It's so soft," he commented.

"You can't do that all night, or I'll combust," I whispered, voice thick with innuendo.

Chance released a husky laugh against my skin, then pulled back slightly, his brow furrowing.

"What?"

"You're missing something."

"I didn't forget anything." Amanda folded her arms over her chest, across the room, but still having heard his comment.

From out of nowhere, Chance produced a square black velvet box.

I shook my head, not liking where this was going.

His grin widened as he opened the box.

Amanda gasped from behind me.

I was simply rendered speechless.

Inside the box was a pair of absolutely breathtaking vintage diamond earrings. Tiny, brilliant stones trailed along the slender frame, leading to three dangling diamonds, the bottom of which was largest and shaped like a teardrop, in a clearly art deco-inspired design.

"Where'd you get those?" Amanda asked in disbelief.

"Mom said Violet could wear them for the night." He beamed at me.

I just kept shaking my head.

"They're perfect with the dress," Amanda commented.

"Chance..."

"Just try them on," he encouraged me.

I swallowed hard, not even wanting to entertain it, but knowing between Chance and his sister, I didn't have much of a choice.

With shaking hands, I removed my simple gold studs, which were half-tarnished and definitely from the clearance rack at some department store. I hesitated for a moment before carefully plucking one earring from the velvet box.

Delicate, intricate, and much lighter than I would have expected, they caught the light with even the smallest movement, radiantly glittering. After fastening both, Chance and Amanda gave an identical cluck of approval, demonstrating their relation.

Amanda's wide smile said more than her words could, and Chance placed another tender kiss at my temple. "You are breathtaking, Violet."

"Thank you," I murmured, my throat suddenly dry.

"Shall we?" Chance extended his hand, palm up, for mine.

I gave a brief nod, slipping my hand in his.

I wondered if he knew I'd follow him anywhere.

Chapter 11

"Cut it out," I hissed, pushing Chance's hand away from stroking the velvet fabric at my thigh for the umpteenth time during dinner.

He gave no reaction, but moments later, his hand was back on my thigh under the table. This man was going to be the end of me.

The ballroom was decked out in silver and emerald decor for the fundraising event. In the dim light of the crystal chandeliers, everything seemed to sparkle. It was magical in its own way and certainly a spectacle of grandeur. Errantly, I wondered if Amanda had meant to dress me to match the color scheme of each event, as I had also suspiciously coordinated with the burgundy and blush theme of the tea party as well.

Beyond the sea of round tables, each covered with fanciful centerpieces made of holiday florals, a small stage had been erected. The four stringed instruments of the Astoria Quartet were awaiting their owners, sitting primly in their stands. Some guests had already taken their seats, while others continued to mingle by the bar or networked throughout the room.

It was a distinctly different crowd from the tea party. You could feel the desperation and aspiration suffusing the room. The men and women present at the fundraiser were the wheelers and dealers of the East Coast elite. I took a deep breath, knowing I was in for a long night.

Once seated, Chance and I found we were assigned to the same round table as Chance's parents, sister, and Hiram, but the other half of the table was occupied by important associates of his father, likely to allow for both strategic conversations and to showcase their significance amongst the point-one-percent crowd in attendance at the fundraising event that evening.

In between the mediocre chicken and never-ending speeches, I was subjected to suffering through posturing and the most ridiculous complaints from Thomas Roberts's associates. The only saving grace was Chance squeezing my thigh when particularly absurd comments were made.

Langston Wellesley, Thomas's political strategist, spent the evening complaining about funding allocations for the donations that came through during the event, and which lobbies they should support in the coming year with said money.

Brock Calloway, Thomas's hedge fund CEO, droned on about the market rates, but made multiple jokes about tax loopholes that had me fuming. His wife, Genevieve, was no better, making snide comments to Cindy about how their yacht renovations were taking too long and the travesty of having to use the spare yacht during the summer in Capri, which she kept pronouncing, "Kaaah-pri," elongating the first syllable awkwardly.

But worst of all was Quintin Devereaux, an obnoxious tech entrepreneur who felt it was necessary to enlighten the table about the plebian lemmings that helped him make his billions by not reading terms and conditions, allowing him to sell their data and amass his fortune. He seemed to equate wealth to intelligence, and gave off absolute slimeball vibes.

"Don't let that creep anywhere near me," I'd whispered to Chance after another of his rants about how he could get anything he wanted, and how easy it was to use money to have people do his bidding.

"I was hoping you'd protect me," he'd snorted derisively.

To my horror, over dessert, conversation somehow found its way around the table to Chance and me.

"Teaching is so noble," Genevieve commented.

I pursed my lips. Clearly, that was a talking point this crowd had for working-class occupations, but there remained an undercurrent of condescension in the choice of words.

"I'm surprised you sent your kids to Montgomery. Would have assumed Preston Academy would have been your preference," Brock teased Thomas.

"They are legacies," Thomas said sternly, seemingly irritated with his alma mater being belittled.

"It's where we met," Cindy told the table brightly. "Montgomery will always be a special place for us, which is why we've been so generous with our donations. I'm so proud that Chance decided to teach there and that he has his own Montgomery love story."

"What does your family think about your profession?" Sleazeball Quintin asked me, his gaze bouncing from my eyes, to my lips, to my breasts, and back up.

I took a beat, weighing my options, because there were a lot of things I could say, and I really wished Chance's parents weren't sitting at the table with us, but recalling the pep talk I'd gotten from Chance the day before in the atrium, after my humiliation at the tea party, I found that I only cared what he thought. And I figured Chance would appreciate the reply I decided on.

"Oh, I'm poor. My mom's probably just happy I'm employed." I beamed at him.

Quintin's expression faltered.

Chance's hand firmly squeezed my leg under the table, and his face began to redden, trying to hold back laughter. At least he appreciated my self-deprecation.

Thomas closed his eyes and took a deep breath. Cindy continued to pick at her dessert absently, pretending that she hadn't heard me at all. The rest of the table went silent for a moment, and then the conversation swiftly moved to a safer topic.

"That is the hottest thing you've ever done," Chance whispered, his breath warm against the shell of my ear. "I'm so fucking in love with you." He slid his hand up higher along my thigh, brushing his fingers over my lap, so close, yet so far, from what he truly wanted.

I grabbed his hand and planted it back in his own lap. "You'll need to wait."

"I love it when you're bossy."

I glared at him, but there was no real venom behind the look.

CHAPTER 12

"Maybe we should go back through the letters for more clues about the whereabouts of the key," Chance suggested, resting his chin on the top of my head, his arms encircling me from behind as we waited for the famed Astoria Quartet to finish setting up and begin to play, closing out the fundraiser with a refined concert fit for the crowd.

"That's fine. Did you get a chance to ask your mom about helping us look at the old photo albums?" I asked.

"No; I couldn't find her while you were getting ready with Amanda. She's been glued to my dad's hip all night, and I don't want him asking questions," he reasoned.

"That's okay." I squeezed his hand. "And you're sure we shouldn't start tilting books, looking for a lever?"

He chuckled behind me, the motion shaking my own body, as my back was resting against him. "Let's leave that for a last resort, Daphne," he joked, referencing Scooby Doo again.

"I identify more with Velma," I retorted.

"You just like arguing with me." He pulled me closer, no doubt wanting me to feel his hardness pressed against my ass. "You know it turns me on."

"You're ridiculous." I huffed a laugh at his antics, secretly appreciating our coded foreplay.

The couple in front of us moved to refresh their drinks at the bar, leaving Chance and me right behind Langston and Brock, who were in the midst of a heated conversation that became audible without a barrier between us.

"I'm worried any incidents might cause an issue with his public image and could crater the stock price," Brock hissed.

"I've already got a running list of suitable replacements, ranked by their value for our strategic alliances," Langston replied, seemingly annoyed with the discussion. "He'll tire of her eventually. We all go through our phases of experimentation well below our pedigree. It won't last."

My blood ran cold, and I heard Chance's breath catch in his throat; his body went rigid against mine.

They were talking about us.

"If you're sure…" Brock sighed.

Langston continued, "Finding an appropriate match for his scion is too important to the perception of the Roberts's name and brand for the investors. You can wrap her up in pretty packaging all you want, but when you fuck trash, you look like trash."

Chance released me and lunged at Langston, shoving him forward. "Shut the fuck up, you piece of shit!"

The crowd went silent.

My heart stopped.

"Chance don't..." I tried to grab him, but he shook me off.

Langston turned around, his eyes wide, as he righted himself and shook off the physical altercation.

"You think you're better than everyone," Chance growled. "You have no fucking idea what it's like with all your champagne problems." He stepped back, gesturing to the crowd that was watching him with rapt attention.

"All of you should be ashamed of yourselves—the way you parade around here, treating people like shit if they aren't in your tax bracket. What gives you the right to judge them? Do you have even a speck of kindness left in your rotten souls? I suppose not, since you can't buy it," he spit.

The room was still so still you could have heard a pin drop.

"Chance, please..." I grabbed his hand, attempting to pull him away with me, but he stood firm.

His gaze returned to Langston. "Apologize to her," he demanded.

Langston's mouth popped open in surprise; his gaze flitted just over my shoulder, with a note of relief entering his expression.

I turned to find Thomas making his way toward us, and before I could do anything, his hand was firmly on Chance's shoulder. "Come now, son. You've had too much to drink. Let's go."

Chance glared at his father with lethal determination. "I haven't had a single sip of alcohol all evening. Don't dismiss me," he stated firmly, then turned his attention back to Langston. "Apologize to the lady for what you said."

Thomas's jaw clenched, but he didn't intervene.

Langston's gaze ping-ponged between Chance, me, and Thomas, before it settled on me. "I apologize, Miss Price," he ground out without an ounce of sincerity, but laced with plenty of indignance over being called out in front of such a prestigious crowd. And that was enough for me.

I released a ragged breath, thinking that the situation was over, but I was mistaken.

Chance took one step forward, placing him inches from Langston's face and requiring the man to tip his head up to meet Chance's eyes. "If I ever hear you speak about her again, you'll regret it." The threat was delivered low but clear.

Fear flashed in Langston's eyes as he swallowed hard.

I'd never seen Chance so worked up. I didn't know what to do. He never lost his cool, not even when his students were being terrors. Part of me felt guilty that I was the reason he'd confronted his father's associates. If I hadn't made that flippant comment at dinner, maybe they wouldn't have been so vicious with their words. But I'd be lying if I said another part wasn't so proud of him for standing his ground, and for standing up for us...for me.

"We're leaving," he told me curtly, pulling my hand along to follow behind him, the crowd parting for us, still gawking at the spectacle he'd caused.

I didn't even want to think about how this would reflect on his family. Making sure Chance was okay was the most important thing. Figuring out if he had just been disowned could wait.

CHAPTER 13

I trailed behind Chance as he stormed up the stairs without a word, ignoring the scandalized murmuring from the ballroom behind us.

Once in our room, he hauled our shared suitcase into the middle of the space and began to haphazardly fling clothing, shoes, and toiletries into the luggage.

"Chance..." I stepped between him and the suitcase, grabbing hold of his biceps with my hands. "Talk to me..."

He dropped the shirt in his hand, the hanger, still threaded through the neck, clattered when it hit the floor. Chance stepped forward, pulling me into a tight hug, burying his face into my neck. His breathing was erratic as he took huge gulping breaths.

"It's okay," I said softly, running my fingers through his hair.

"I hate them," he growled, his body trembling in my arms. "I hate them all."

"It's just us, love," I cooed. "Just us."

"I can't lose you," he replied hoarsely.

"I'm right here," I assured him, rubbing wide circles across his back. "I'm not going anywhere." I took a step back, placing my hands on either side of his face, forcing him to look me in the eyes.

The fact that it had even crossed his mind that it was possible for him to lose me was baffling. Was it not obvious to him that I was the lucky one? He was everything to me—my support, my courage, my heart.

The only other time I'd seen him this emotional was when he'd found me in the basement offices at the school, fighting for my life. "I'm too stubborn to leave you," I told him.

The corner of his mouth lifted almost imperceptibly.

"We're okay," I asserted, pulling his face to mine for a quick peck. "Are you okay?"

Chance swallowed. "I just saw red..."

He looked devastated. Did he think what happened was going to scare me off?

How could he think that anything they said would change a single thing between us? Nobody understood the connection we shared. It was beyond their capacity to see the depth of our love.

"They deserved it." I smiled at him, caressing his cheek softly.

"They deserved worse," he grumbled.

The tender notes of the string quartet floated into the room through the door that had been left open in our haste, pausing our conversation.

"You were looking forward to the concert." Chance frowned.

I gave him a mischievous smile, causing his brow to furrow, before pulling him into the hallway. The lighting had been dimmed in the wide, marble-clad passage, cascading a nebulous glow along and through the glittering crystal of the chandeliers lining the ceiling the span of the space. It was like we had our own private hall, complete with twinkling starlight above us.

"Dance with me." I grinned at Chance, wrapping one arm around his waist and pulling our clasped hands between us, then laying my head against his chest.

With a contented sigh, Chance settled against me, tugging me even closer as we swayed to the music. I don't know how long we stayed like that, just soaking in the lilting notes and taking in each other's warmth. I would have stayed with him, safe in his embrace, forever.

I hated how the people, just below us, made Chance feel inferior. Their rules and elitism trapped people within their system of superiority. Chance had been born into their world, but he was never enough. And even after making the decision to forge his own path, he was still condemned as a disappointment.

The way they made him feel made my stomach churn. He tried so fucking hard to be his best self. He was passionate, kind, gentle, and generous. They had no idea who he was, but they judged him all the same. It was a wonder that someone like him, with so much goodness, was able to come from a system that punished those who would put others above themselves, unless it came with a press release and an award recognizing such charitable works.

He was right to tell them they should be ashamed of themselves.

"I like this much better—just the two of us," I told him.

"I love you, Violet," he whispered. "I love you so much it hurts. Every breath I take is for and because of you. You are everything."

I blinked back tears as I tilted my head up to look at Chance...to really look at him. This man filled in a piece of me that I didn't know existed, but one that had ached for years. He had given me purpose, and strength, and light. "*You* are everything," I told him softly, bringing my palm up to cup his cheek, gently drawing him to me.

And when his lips met mine, the music faded into the background along with everything else. It was always like this when it was just Chance and me. Nothing else mattered. There was only him.

I'd fought it for a long time, but having surrendered almost a year before, it felt so easy to let him in now. It was easy to give him everything, because he'd done the same for me.

Our kiss was long and languid, a prelude to what was to come. He sucked and stroked so tenderly, it was effortless to get lost in him. The connection we had was so palpable in moments like that, it felt as if I could reach out and touch it...be wrapped up in it, like a warm embrace.

It wasn't when the music ended, but rather when there was a burst of applause at the end of the concert that Chance and I returned to our surroundings.

"Let me take you to bed." His words were a husky purr in my ear.

I merely nodded in agreement, making sure to lock the bedroom door behind us.

Normally, Chance and I were quite verbal leading up to and during any sexual activities, but that evening, it felt more right to simply feel each other and experience the moments, basking in the soft noises, rather than teasing one another.

Chance came around behind me, his fingers immediately unzipping my dress, the fabric sighing as it slipped off my shoulders, forming a green velvet pool at my feet, which I neatly stepped out of, turning to regard Chance in nothing but a black seamless thong, the necklace he had gifted me last New Year's, and my borrowed diamond earrings.

He swallowed as his eyes roved over me, a hunger visible just beneath the surface.

With a knowing smile, I reached forward and unfastened the bow tie of his tuxedo, tossing it to the ground after slipping it from his collar.

He watched me intently, eyes burning with desire, his breath coming out in short pants as I took my time undressing him. I was impressed that his hands remained at his sides, although occasionally I would catch a finger twitching with impatience.

When Chance was in nothing but his underwear, I slid mine off first, receiving an appreciative smirk from him, before I hooked my fingers in the elastic of his boxer briefs and made quick work of removing them, allowing his erection to spring free.

Taking Chance's fingers in mine, I led him over to the bed, gently pushing him to sit at the edge of the mattress. He raised a single brow with curiosity as he followed my direction, but released a knowing groan when I sank down to my knees in front of him, placing my palms on his knees and pushing them apart to make room for my body between them.

Wasting no time, I leaned forward, wrapping my lips around the head of his cock, earning a loud hiss from Chance above me. With one hand braced on his thigh, and the other at the base of his cock, I alternated between swirling my tongue around what I could fit in my mouth and hollowing my cheeks to suck him in farther.

After a year of experimentation with Chance, I'd figured out this combination was his favorite. His groans spurred me forward, and I felt myself becoming slick as a result of his pleasure.

"Fuck, baby..." he moaned as he neared his climax. I gently squeezed his balls, one after another.

Getting him off was this whole other level of accomplishment for me. Chance was a generous lover, and he'd never once asked for reciprocation, but I rather enjoyed seeing him unravel at my hand...or mouth, in this case.

Hearing his breath hitch, I released him and used my hand to bring him to completion, our hooded gazes locked on one another as he came on my chest. Chance had never judged me or complained about me not wanting to swallow his release, which meant more to me than he could know, as I'd been pressured by every partner before him.

"Your turn, muse." He gave me a satiated smile as he helped me to my feet. His gaze turned dark as he watched me crawl up onto the bed, before he followed me, quickly finding his favorite position, resting on his stomach with his face buried between my thighs.

It wasn't fair that he was so talented with his tongue, really.

If he knew how often I thought about how skilled his mouth was, I'd never hear the end of it. Instead, I gave in to the sensation of his worshipping touches, bucking against his teasing patterns, soft one moment and hard the next. Chance delighted in my tortured keening, but eventually took pity on me and allowed me to find my own release.

When I discovered that he was hard again, I shoved him down onto the mattress, eliciting an amused chuckle from Chance, who enjoyed it when I took charge. "I want to ride you," I told him, swinging one leg over his thighs to straddle him.

It was easy for him to slide in; I was soaked as a result of our mutual oral exchange.

We released a unified sigh of relief when he was seated inside me, as if it was where he was always meant to be...because it was.

His hands came up to cup my breasts, tweaking my nipples when he wanted my attention, as I rocked against him. But I found I couldn't get close enough to him. I leaned down, our chests colliding as I continued to roll my hips in rhythm with his. Our kisses became rough and sloppy as we neared another climax.

Impatient as he was, Chance reached between us, easily locating my clit and helping me find my release so he could come inside me a moment later, our panting breaths the only sound other than our wildly beating hearts against one another.

There was nothing in the world that made more sense than being with Chance, connected so intimately...mind, body, and soul. When we were together, everything and everyone else simply ceased to exist.

Tuesday, December 21

CHAPTER 14

"Is there such a thing as an emotional hangover?" Chance groaned into my neck the next morning.

"Definitely," I rasped.

Thankfully, we'd been allowed to sleep in after the previous night's fiasco. The room was an absolute mess as a result of Chance abandoning his rushed attempt at packing up and leaving.

"I hope I didn't upset my mom..." he worried.

"She'll understand," I replied, combing my fingers through his hair. His entire body was wrapped around me like a boa constrictor. I loved it.

I couldn't remember anyone standing up for me like Chance had the night before, and if there was anything remaining of my internal walls, surely they'd been demolished last night after his so very public demonstration of support.

"You're a terrible influence," he moaned, "I don't want to get up. I used to be a morning person before I met you."

I turned in his arms and placed a kiss on his chin. "But sleeping in is the best, and I find ways to make it worth your while..." I concluded suggestively.

His gaze sizzled.

So an hour later, after Chance kept me waylaid in bed, we finally decided that it would be advantageous to get up and procure some coffee and breakfast while we strategized over the letters once more.

"We know that at some point she moved the key from her bedroom to the drawing room, most likely, but I wonder if we can find something that indicates where in the room she might have hidden the key. The drawing room is huge," I said, spreading the letters out on the bed, keeping them far enough away from the tray of coffee and breakfast food someone had brought up, at Chance's request. "Am I nuts for thinking it might still be where she left it?" I sighed.

Chance cocked his head at me, "If anyone can find it, it's you. Your determination knows no bounds."

I gave him a small smile, appreciative of his support. "You're kind to humor me."

He returned the sentiment with a devilish grin. "There's nowhere else I would rather be than indulging your curiosity."

For the next few hours, well into the afternoon, we continued to pore over the letters, examining every small line, searching for anything that might reveal where Mitzi could have hidden the key in the drawing room.

And just before Amanda came to retrieve me to prepare for the evening event, I found exactly what we were looking for.

"It's in a clock!" I exclaimed, startling Chance, who jumped at the volume of my voice, laughing sheepishly at himself a moment later.

I handed him the letter.

"The second-to-last paragraph."

The only thing that allowed me to make it through listening to the Sedgewick sisters droning on was watching the time, willing the minutes to move faster, just for the chance to see you again. If they only knew the secrets that little clock holds.

His eyebrows raised as he read the passage, a victorious smile curled his lips, "I think you've found it, muse."

"You guys are such nerds, doing schoolwork over Christmas break," Amanda teased from the doorway, her eyes trained on the papers strewn all over the bed. "I'm here to collect my ward." Her gaze landed on me.

My shoulders slumped.

"Our mission will have to wait." I grimaced.

I was so thankful for Amanda's skill and eye for fashion. I was hopeless, usually dressing in all black, when I wasn't stuck in slacks and a button-up for work at the school.

For the charity auction and marketplace, she had chosen for me a bloodred floor-length gown made of silk, with a crossover halter-neckline that showcased just the right amount of cleavage, leaving my lean clavicle and shoulders bare.

She instructed her hair stylist to pull my normally wavy brown hair into a sleek and straight ponytail, and requested that I wear a red lipstick to complement the dress.

"I can't guarantee it won't be all over my teeth by the end of the night." I sighed in defeat as her makeup artist paused while lining my lips.

"Just don't go making out with my brother until after the event is done, okay?" Amanda instructed.

I rolled my eyes, but a smile remained on my lips.

"I was able to snag another rental from Mom for you," Amanda changed the subject as she sorted through a few stacked boxes on the sideboard in her room, pulling a much larger square velvet box from the pile than those which had contained the beautiful earrings Chance had borrowed on my behalf the night before.

Amanda propped open the box as she approached me. "This one's Victorian." Her voice matched the coy expression upon her face.

The gold and diamond cuff bracelet gently sitting against the black velvet cushion inside the box didn't look like something a person wore—it looked like something that would be displayed in a museum, behind glass, with a placard explaining that it had been worn by a long list of various and long-forgotten female dignitaries.

The golden lattice of filigree was spun so delicately, it could have been stitched from light. Even the slightest movement caught on the scattered diamonds embedded within the design, allowing the small stones to flicker and flare like stars. I didn't even want to breathe on it, let alone wear it all evening.

"What if one of the stones comes loose?" I argued, taking a small step back from Amanda.

"They won't." She chuckled, closing the space between us and grabbing for my wrist before I could get away. "Is it terrible that I think it's funny how allergic you are to nice things?"

"Ha ha," I deadpanned, watching her with a scowl as she fastened the bracelet to my wrist.

Like the earrings, the bracelet was much lighter than I had anticipated, but the gold tone looked brilliant against the deep red of the dress.

To my dismay, Amanda procured another small box with a pair of dainty gold earrings. "These are just from Saks," she told me. "We'll start with one family heirloom piece per outfit and work you up to more." Her broad grin told me she was teasing.

"Did Chance put you up to this?" I huffed a laugh.

"No, darling." She squeezed my hand. "Just want you looking your best while you swim through the sea of sharks downstairs."

The thought was sobering.

Sensing my discord, she continued, "Think of it as playing dress-up if you want. Every woman deserves to look their best. And I love getting to see you sparkle and shine."

Amanda was such a beacon of light. The first moment I'd met her last year, she'd taken me under her wing. Never judging, only ever offering grace and sincerity. I would never forget her kindness. Because I loved her brother, she loved me. It was that simple.

When Chance arrived with Hiram a while later to escort us downstairs, he once again looked terribly debonair in a perfectly tailored suit and was obsessed with the fabric of my dress.

"This one's even softer than the green one," he murmured, fingering the fabric along the hem of the back of my dress, tickling the bare skin beneath it in the process.

"I'm going to kill you. Cut it out," I hissed.

"You're already killing me, muse," he replied suavely, but did relent with his caresses for the moment. "Come along. Amanda said Mom is waiting for us downstairs with instructions."

"Instructions?" I questioned. "She's not mad about last night, is she?"

"No." Chance shook his head as we made our way down the upstairs hallway to the grand staircase. "Trust me, everyone will pretend it never happened."

"You're sure?" I faltered, stopping him just before we reached the top of the staircase.

He tipped his head down to meet my gaze. "They won't have forgotten, and they may whisper in your wake, but nobody will say anything to you," he tried to assure me.

His eyes lingered on my mouth a beat too long. "Amanda says I can't kiss you," he grumbled.

I shook my head.

Chance sighed. "It's going to be a long night."

And just as the words left his mouth, I spotted Simone at the coat check, with a glass of champagne already in hand. "I might need to employ you as a wine shield this evening."

Chance huffed and shook his head as he followed my gaze and saw Simone for himself. "I've got a better plan. How about I whisper the most filthy things in your ear all night, leaving you in a perpetual state of blushing, so whenever she looks at you, she knows exactly how obsessed I am with you?"

As if he'd spoken it into existence, I felt my cheeks heat.

"You wouldn't dare," I breathed.

"You know better than to issue me a challenge, muse." He chuckled.

Saved from further embarrassment, I was pleased to find Cindy waiting for us at the bottom of the stairs. "Aren't you two just a vision." She smiled warmly, taking both of us in the way only a proud mother can.

"Amanda said you had instructions," Chance reminded her.

"Oh, yes!" Her face lit up. She reached into her purse and pulled out a wad of hundred-dollar bills, discreetly giving them to Chance. "It's important that we set a good example for our guests. I need you each to make at least one purchase in the marketplace to show our support."

Chance nodded. My throat went dry.

"Also"—she directed her attention to Chance—"you need to win something in the silent auction. I'll pay, but use your name. Whatever you want."

He nodded. My chest felt tight.

"Oh," she noted, almost as if it was an afterthought, "and one of the celebrities had to drop out of the charity auction." She told Chance. "I'll need you to fill in for him and offer up a photography lesson or portrait session."

Chance's mouth parted in surprise. My hand tightened around his.

Cindy's eyes found mine. "I don't want you to worry. It's just a formality. Sometimes the bidders don't even end up using what they've won."

"Mom…" Chance's voice was worried.

She looked over at her son. "It'll be fine. Just trust me."

He glanced down at me.

All I could think to do was shrug. She never asked anything of him, and we'd made a spectacle of ourselves the night before. I supposed it was the least he could do.

"Fine," he surrendered. "Is that everything?"

She smiled again. "Have fun!" And with that, she disappeared into the crowd.

"I'm sorry," he offered.

"She asked us to trust her, and I do," I told him.

He gave a brief nod in agreement, glancing through the throng of people milling about on the main floor. "Let's see if we can find the most expensive thing to force you to buy."

I just about choked in response, which only delighted Chance.

CHAPTER 15

As I had suspected, my attire once again appeared to be synchronous with the event decor. For the third event of the Winter Revelry, everything had been redecorated in brilliant shades of red and gold, with velvet ruby sashing swooping along the corners of each doorway, and the trees decked in sparkling gold ornaments, glittering red ribbon, and twinkling warm white lights that twinkled in harmony. It was stunning, but all I could think about was how many people it had taken to redecorate, night after night.

"I know we said no Christmas presents this year, but maybe it shouldn't count if it's not our money?" Chance suggested as we slowly made our way through the charity marketplace that had been set up, spanning multiple rooms on the first floor, each themed with different categories of vendors.

While the entrance hall was busy with arriving guests grabbing drinks and hors d'oeuvres as they checked their coats, the rest of the house was positively buzzing with the crowd excitedly shopping among the dozens of vendors Cindy had brought in.

The drawing room was filled with fine jewelry and watches, while the music room next door displayed couture and vintage fashion and accessories. The wide hallways off the grand entrance hall, which Chance referred to as the gallery, were crammed full with artwork for sale, while the game room featured luxury linens, stationery, and children's gifts. Fittingly, there were artisanal and gourmet food baskets and dining experiences available for perusal in the dining room, the items in the smoking room seemed to be gifts more tailored for gentlemen, and of course, the library was showcasing rare books and collectables.

It was so overwhelming, I didn't know where to start, and truthfully, it didn't feel right to spend any of Cindy's money. If Chance noticed me spending a second longer looking at something, he'd suggest we get it, and if I huffed about it, he reminded me to think of the money as going to charity, rather than coming from his family, as a large portion of the proceeds from the marketplace would be donated.

"What do you think about these for Amanda?" Chance pointed to a beautiful pair of round solitaire diamond earrings that had a similar cut to the necklace he'd given me from his grandmother.

"She may already have something similar…" I bit my lip. I'd talked to Amanda so much, but I didn't know her well enough to be able to say what kind of jewelry she'd prefer, although I did know what colors and fabrics she preferred for her clothing.

"She mentioned she was thinking about getting a pair she could use for travel." He leaned in closer to examine the earrings in the case. "Do you have a smaller pair?" he asked the attendant.

The woman was delighted at the question and pulled up a cushion from beneath the display, placing another set that was half the size on the glass countertop. "These are half a carat each. Solesfera cut. Flawless clarity. Twenty-four carat gold. You won't find a more brilliant cut in the room."

Chance glanced at me. "Do you like them?"

I narrowed my eyes at him. "This better not be a trick."

He chuckled. "Just tell me if you like them."

"Of course I do. They're beautiful. She'll love them." I huffed.

Chance beamed at me, pulling me in to place a kiss at my temple before handing a card to the attendant. I didn't want to know how much they cost, and I hoped he'd been truthful with me.

I was trying to find a balance when it came to Chance's generosity. I recognized that it made him happy to spoil me and take care of me in his own way. I just needed to make sure that I showed him my appreciation and that he never felt as though his kindness was being taken for granted.

Chance gleefully accepted the tiny bag from the attendant, grabbing my hand with the other. "Now you just have to find something so we can report back to my mom that this part of our mission has been completed."

I'd always struggled with gift ideas for Chance, not only because I still had no budget while I tried to aggressively pay off my student loans, but also because he usually just bought himself anything he wanted. I had to think outside of the box and get creative with ideas, but I wasn't very crafty or imaginative, so I had my work cut out for me.

We were on our second loop through the rooms when I spotted what I hoped would be the perfect option. "I think I found something," I told Chance, my tone tentative.

He raised a brow in delight.

"I want it to be a surprise," I told him.

Catching my drift, he discreetly passed me some of the cash his mother had given him. "Will that be enough?"

"If it isn't, I won't get it." I guffawed, looking down at the five hundred-dollar bills neatly folded in my palm.

"I'll wait for you by the door." He pointed to the entrance of the game room. "Don't get into trouble."

"Hopefully no other wine glasses find themselves in my lap." I gave him an artificially large smile.

He just shook his head and turned for the door.

Making my way over to the booth, I politely waited my turn while the attendant finished up with another customer. Hanging on neat wooden racks were beautiful handmade ornaments that could be customized with text, if desired.

"I'm interested in that one." I pointed to one with a lovely scene of a cozy fireplace next to a window with snow gently falling outside. The painted image looked almost exactly like the lounge, where Chance and I had fallen in love.

I was a little squeamish when the attendant relayed the price. It would be less than a hundred, and I supposed it was hand-painted and sentimental. So I handed over a bill, instructing the attendant to keep the change as a tip, to which he smiled with sincere appreciation.

As I instructed, he inscribed the delicate little ornament with the previous year in neat script writing, right before my eyes. Afterwards, I watched him pack the ornament with great care in multiple layers to keep it safe and sound and thanked him before finding Chance waiting for me.

"No wine spilled. I'd call that a victory." He leaned down to kiss me, but swerved to my cheek at the last moment, having briefly forgotten his directive from Amanda not to smudge my red lipstick.

I returned the rest of the money to him, and although I still felt a pang of guilt over having spent someone else's money, and so much of it, on something so small, Chance's cheerful mood made me feel better. And, truly, I was excited to give him the gift, commemorating our actual first Christmas together.

CHAPTER 16

Next, we made our way into the ballroom, where dinner and the auction would be taking place. Lining the room were tables for the silent auction, each with an easel describing the prize up for grabs and a clipboard with names and bids.

Some of the items up for auction were seriously unbelievable. Tons of vacations and adventures all over the world, trips on mega yachts, a year's worth of flights with a private jet company, but also experiences that I'd never even considered could be gifted, like private concerts with big-name musicians, lunches with celebrities, set visits, naming characters in books or films—it was astonishing.

There were also various one-of-a-kind items available, like musical instruments, signed sports paraphernalia, first edition books, movie scripts, and even a few antiquities that were fascinating, but I had to wonder if the provided provenance was legitimate.

"Should we bid on this Egyptian figurine?" Chance noted when I'd stopped to look at the small bust.

I shook my head. "There's no way that came here legally. It belongs in a museum, in Egypt, not in a private collection halfway around the world." I huffed.

"We could liberate it," he offered sincerely.

"Better not."

A little while later, Chance seemed to have found what he wanted to bid on, but wouldn't share. "I let you surprise me; give me a turn," he pleaded.

And who was I to refuse when he'd asked so nicely?

"Fine, I'll find our table," I relayed begrudgingly.

I was pleased to find that Amanda and Hiram were again seated with us, and the other placards included his parents, but an entirely different set of guests than from the evening before. Hopefully this dinner wouldn't be as much of a spectacle.

"Where's Chance?" Amanda asked as Hiram stood to help me take my seat.

I gave him a smile in gratitude. "Staking out something in the silent auction." I tipped my head toward the corner of the room where he was trying to scare off any potential competition for whatever he wanted to bid on so badly.

Amanda giggled.

Not long after, guests were asked to take their seats and the silent auction was called to a close. Chance took his seat with a smug grin, having secured his secret prize.

"What'd you win?" I nudged Chance.

"You'll see." He smirked.

Thankfully, the other guests seated at our table were a distinctly different crowd from the fundraiser the night before. I had to wonder if this had been the original seating arrangement, or if adjustments had been made after the scene Chance and I had inadvertently caused.

This time, it was mostly women, who seemed to be familiar with Cindy through her charity work—likely other donors. The couple that sat next to Thomas, on the opposite side of Cindy, seemed to be the only people who weren't part of the charity scene and made polite but indiscernible conversation with him while we ate dinner and watched the auction.

The MC was a gregarious woman who alternated between the live auction and announcing the highest bids on the silent auction items. After each, the winner was called to the stage for a photo op and obligatory hand shaking. Occasionally there would be hoots and hollers from the crowd if they were particularly pleased with the winners, or teasing boos when someone lost an auction to a friend.

The live auction grew increasingly animated as the dinner wore on and more drinks were consumed by the generous crowd.

Someone from the staff came to retrieve Chance when it was his turn to go up on stage while they auctioned off his photography services; however, just before he got up from the table, his name was called for another reason.

According to the MC, he had won an all-expenses-paid trip for two to a private villa in Greece for a two-week excursion, complete with private travel arrangements, and a staff.

My lips parted in shock at the extravagance of it all.

"Surprise," he whispered, placing a kiss at my temple before making his way to the stage to claim his victory.

There was no way he planned on us taking that trip. I reached for my glass to take a sip and ease my nerves at the thought. Because in my heart, I knew he had. We'd often talked about how going to Greece to see the classical history I had studied and taught for years, in real life, was my dream. I couldn't help but be a little smitten at his thoughtfulness.

"Won't that be a nice honeymoon?" Cindy patted my arm.

I just about choked on the champagne. She was getting a little ahead of herself.

After graciously accepting his silent auction prize, the MC began to talk him up to the crowd.

"We have in our midst an award-winning and world-renowned photographer, Mr. Chance Harper, and up for bid is a private photography session, which can be used for an individual, family, or organization," she touted.

I couldn't help but beam at him, our eyes connecting through the room. He indeed had won an award for one of his portraits of me at the show he'd just returned from, in Edinburgh. And I guess it was an international award, so now I had more fodder to tease him about. Ever humble, nothing made Chance blush more than me lavishing him with praise for his beautiful photographic work.

"Shall we start the bidding at one thousand?" the MC asked.

Multiple paddles rose, and the race began.

Cindy leaned over. "Would you mind bidding on my behalf?"

I turned to look at her, my brow furrowed, surprised by the request.

"He'll be cross with me if his own mother outbids everyone, but he won't mind if it's you." She smiled at me...a smile she shared with Chance, and one that I found very difficult to refuse.

"If you need photos, he'll take them for free," I said in a hushed tone, while the bids continued to rise.

"Nonsense." She waved a hand. "It's for a good cause, and I've been meaning to get some updated headshots." She placed her paddle on the table and slid it toward me.

Tentatively, I reached out to take it in my hand. It was thin, made of a light balsa wood, with big, bold black numbers: 125. "Okay," I replied nervously.

"I'll tap your arm when I'd like for you to bid."

I gave her a nervous nod. I'd only ever seen auctions on TV. I was worried I was going to mess this up for Cindy, and then Chance would get stuck taking photos for some awful blue blood.

"Twenty thousand," a firm but feminine voice declared across the room, requesting to raise the bidding price higher than the standard increments.

I looked over. Speaking of awful blue bloods, the bidder was none other than Simone Charles.

My eyes shot to Chance, who was trying his hardest not to show his annoyance. Despite the attempt, his lips were pressed in a firm line, eyes narrowed at Simone.

"Wonderful! Twenty thousand for the beautiful redhead. Do I hear twenty-five?"

Cindy tapped my arm. "Bid, please," she requested warmly.

I didn't know how, but she'd known that Simone was going to bid. Understanding that Cindy saw through the woman who had not only been cruel, but who had humiliated me at the tea party, settled something inside me I hadn't realized was discontented.

In her own way, this was how Cindy was able to punish Simone for what she'd done, and in doing so, she was also standing up for me in the process...as if I were one of her own. And I realized at that moment, I wanted to be.

Without another thought, my arm shot up into the air.

Both the MC and Chance's attention swung to me, their eyes simultaneously flaring with delight, for completely different reasons.

I glanced across the room to Simone, who was still standing, and very obviously shooting a death glare in my direction.

"Do I hear thirty thousand?" the MC asked.

Eyes still on me, Simone raised her paddle again.

And just as before, Cindy tapped my arm, which I shot up defiantly.

The bids ping-ponged back and forth between the two of us for a few rounds, until we reached fifty thousand. God, that kind of money didn't even sound real to me. How on earth had I found myself in this position?

When my paddle went up to raise it to fifty-five, at Cindy's direction, Simone faltered for the first time. She leaned down to talk to the person sitting next to her at the table, an older man with her same red hair, only flecked with greying strands, perhaps her father. He rolled his eyes at whatever she was saying, then firmly shook his head.

"Fifty-five going once," the MC announced.

Simone continued to argue with her father, who stood his ground, her face growing red as he refused her.

"Going twice."

Jaw clenched and lips pursed, she plopped down in her seat and folded her hands over her chest, shoving her father away when he tried to place a comforting hand on her shoulder.

"Sold to bidder 125!" the MC proclaimed. "Come to the stage to collect your photographer."

The crowd laughed at her joke.

"Go on, dear," Cindy prodded me.

I blanched. "It was your bid."

"Go collect your photographer." She laughed.

I felt my cheeks heat as I made my way across the room up to the podium, with everyone watching me. Thankfully, it was Chance who awaited me.

"C'mon, Mr. Award-Winning, World-Renowned Photographer," I teased, trying to play off my nerves as I met Chance up on stage and reached out to him.

But when he took my hand, he didn't follow me. Instead, he pulled me in, dipping me dramatically before I even realized what was happening, and then his lips met mine in an obscenely public display of affection, which I would be forever embarrassed about, much to his delight.

"I'm going to murder you in your sleep," I hissed as he pulled back, his lips ever so slightly stained from my red lipstick. The crowd cheering almost drowned out my threat.

"Worth it," Chance replied, a smug smile plastered across his stupidly handsome face.

WEDNESDAY, DECEMBER 22

CHAPTER 17

"What do you mean the drawing room is closed!?" I growled at the staff member standing guard outside the doors. I'd gotten up early to try to check before the event started, a clear demonstration of my devotion to our cause.

"Violet." Chance squeezed my hand, attempting to reason with me.

It had been a full day since we'd surmised Mitzi's key had been hidden in a clock in the drawing room. But just after we'd figured it out, I'd been whisked away by Amanda to get ready for the auction, and by the time we'd gotten downstairs, the drawing room had been packed full of vendors and guests.

We could have stayed up late to wait them out, but while some of these rich assholes knew how to hold their liquor, they didn't seem to know it was polite to leave on time.

I was determined to look in that room.

"I'll just be a moment." I plastered on a fake smile and did my best entitled-rich-girl impression.

"Santa and his elves are getting ready for the children." The girl crossed her arms over her chest defiantly. "You'll have to wait until ten when the event begins and Santa is ready for visitors."

I clenched my jaw, ready to dig in, but when Chance's arm wrapped around my waist, pulling me into him, I felt my body relax. "Let's go get you some coffee and breakfast, and then we'll come back," he said.

The girl's gaze was fixed on me, trying to decide how much of a fight I was going to put up.

But coffee sounded so much better than arguing with a teenager.

"Fine," I pouted, then turned my gaze back to the girl, pointing a finger in her direction. "But I *will* be back," I promised.

She rolled her eyes as Chance dragged me away toward the kitchen.

"C'mon, tiger." He chuckled.

Ten minutes later, with a full cup of coffee in my stomach alongside some eggs and bacon, even I had to admit I was feeling much less murderous.

"Better?" Chance nudged me.

"Yes," I grumbled, picking at the eggs that were left on my plate.

"You going to apologize to that girl when you see her again?" he asked through a smile.

"Probably." I scowled.

Chance kissed my cheek, a huff of laughter following. "You're so cute when you're cranky in the morning."

The part of me I was fighting in therapy to quiet wondered when he'd get sick of putting up with me. A second voice, from Dr. Short, followed up by asking, "But what if he doesn't? What if he loves you for exactly who you are, flaws and all?"

Chance wrapped his arm around my shoulder, resting his chin on my head. "These letters are almost a hundred years old, Vi. We are going to try our best to see if we can find anything, but we also need to prepare for the idea that we might leave here on Saturday having uncovered nothing at all."

How did he always know what was really bothering me? It was like his superpower.

"I need to know what happened to them." I set my fork down, looking up at him. "I don't care about the secret room. They were so in love, but she didn't end up with him, and I need to know why."

I knew that on a fundamental level, their situation wasn't the same as Chance's and mine. The only similarity was our class differences. Their genders and the stricter societal rules had greatly affected their circumstances.

The failure of their relationship should not have been an indicator of what could happen between Chance and me, but still, I felt drawn to their story. Reading their letters made me yearn for them to find a way to be together.

Their love was so pure, and the way they felt about each other...that felt like how I cared for Chance, with such a ferocity I'd never wanted to fight for someone or something more in my life. He was this integral part of me that was required to function. I needed him to breathe. Just like Mitzi had said in one of her letters, my heart beat only to find its echo in his. Chance's unwavering affection for me had changed me to my core. Damn him, but there simply was no going back to who I had been before. And he knew that. He fucking relished the thought.

"I love you," I whispered into his chest. Sometimes I felt like Chance had found a way to crack my heart right open and build a nest inside. I still didn't understand how he had managed to affix himself to me so permanently.

"I love you too, Violet." He kissed the top of my head. "We'll exhaust every avenue so at the very least we can leave here knowing we tried our best, okay?"

"Okay." I nodded against him.

CHAPTER 18

"You're sure your mom's outside?" I glared at Chance as I threw on the long cream winter coat Amanda had left out for me that morning.

We'd decided that if we couldn't get into the drawing room, the next best thing would be to find Cindy to ask for access to the photo albums in his father's study for us, so we could follow that lead while we waited for access to the room.

Thankfully, my outfit was much more practical, given the day's event was a children's festival. I was all warm and cozy in jeans that fit suspiciously well, brown riding boots, and a gorgeous plum sweater that was softer than anything I'd ever worn before. "It's cashmere," Chance had offered when I'd told him to feel how soft it was.

"That's what the event planner said," Chance replied, wrapping a chunky light brown scarf, speckled with small threads of varying colors, around my neck. "Even though they have space heaters outside in the different activity areas, it's still chilly out."

"I like it when you fuss over me." I grinned up at him as he pulled a knit hat over my head. It matched the scarf, and was complete with a purple pom-pom at the tip in the exact same shade as my sweater.

He placed a soft kiss on the tip of my nose, beaming at me, before handing me a pair of gloves to put on, so he could throw on his own winter gear.

Outside had been transformed into a veritable winter wonderland. The brilliant white sheets of snow beyond the giant patio, where most of the activities were located, certainly helped with the ambiance.

Hand in hand, Chance and I walked through the throngs of children and their parents, looking for Cindy, not that I knew how we'd find her with so many people, all of whom were decked out in their own winter wear.

The snow castle contest was in full swing when we passed by, children of all ages hastily packing snow into various shapes and designs. Holiday music jingled in the background, and there were multiple food stands with all sorts of holiday treats.

"Can we get some hot chocolate?" I asked Chance.

"Of course, baby." He pulled me along toward the line.

"What color coat does your mom have?" I asked him as we waited.

Chance frowned. "I'm sure she has one in every color to suit her outfit or mood."

Just as well. Even if we knew exactly what she was wearing, it was still like looking at a Where's Waldo illustration, but made worse because you were at ground level. I supposed we could have tried to look from above in one of the rooms, but even if we'd spotted her, surely she would have moved by the time we'd have raced back outside.

"Do you have walkie-talkies?" I asked Chance.

"What?" He choked on a laugh.

"Never mind." I shook my head.

After getting our drinks, we continued to scour the area for signs of Cindy. Occasionally, we'd spot a staff member or someone Chance recognized and ask them if they'd seen her, but had no luck.

"We could go ice skating," Chance suggested as we watched children with the animals in the petting zoo. There was even a reindeer, but he was in a separate pen and wasn't able to get pets. Still, the children were in wonder over the animal.

"I want to reopen discussions over getting a pet." I ignored his proposal.

Chance cocked his head. "The conversation has never been closed; there just hasn't been a good time."

"Now's a good time," I told him. "I want a dog. Not too big. Not too small. And it needs to come from a shelter. I want to give one a home that doesn't have one."

Using his gloved hand, he tucked my hair into my scarf, out of my face. "What will the dog do while we're at school all day?"

"We can get a dog walker. Or maybe Mrs. Elwood would check in on it for us." She was an elderly neighbor who was sweet as pie and often talked about a dog she used to have years ago and how she wanted to get another one herself.

"Dogs cost money. Would you insist on paying for half of all the expenses, like how you prefer to split everything else, or would you let me take care of things? If it's the former, how will you reallocate your budget?" he asked.

I pursed my lips. I had thought of that, but hadn't come to a good conclusion. "I don't know yet." I stared up at him.

"Just think about it, and if you make a decision, we can continue to negotiate," he offered.

"Do you want a pet?" I asked him. I'd been the one to keep pushing the issue, and I thought he wanted one, but he'd never straight up said so.

"I want you to be happy." He smiled softly.

"You didn't answer the question."

He sighed. "You know I'm not opposed, but I want to figure things out first."

"Still not an answer."

"I don't think I'll know until we find the right one for us." It wasn't exactly a direct answer, but I did have faith that if he was against it, he would have been honest with me when I'd started asking about the idea.

"Okay." I nodded, accepting his reply. And then, without permission, another question slipped past my lips, one that I hadn't meant to ask aloud. "And what about those?" I gestured to the children surrounding us.

Chance raised an eyebrow. We hadn't had this conversation before. And having it now wasn't exactly the best idea, but it was too late to take it back.

"I don't know..." he replied hesitantly. "Do you?"

Because of how challenging things had been with my mom, I'd ruled out the idea of children for a long time. And I still wasn't sure about my feelings, but I did know that while that door had previously been firmly shut, if Chance wanted to open it, I wouldn't be opposed, exactly. I knew he'd be the right partner to have kids with.

"I don't know either," I admitted.

He exhaled loudly, his shoulders slumping in relief. He knew this could easily be a deal-breaker in any relationship. "That's a much bigger conversation."

"Maybe we can decide after we get a dog." I tried to lighten the mood.

The corner of his lips pulled up into a smile. "Yeah, that sounds like a good idea."

In a weird way, it comforted me that he was on the fence. I knew that we'd make the decision together, and whatever we decided, it would be right for us.

"Sorry…" I mumbled, feeling bad about having brought the conversation to an awkward place.

"No, don't apologize." He tugged me into him for a hug. "We need to think about these things. I will love you no matter what we decide. Dog. No dog. Kids. No kids. It's still you and me at the end of the day, and that's what's most important."

I nodded against him, appreciative of his thoughtfulness and open-minded attitude toward everything. He found a compromise in even the most challenging of situations and was always considerate of my feelings in the process.

"So, ice skating?" he asked.

"I think I've gotten too much attention already this week. I don't need a bunch of kids laughing at me when I fall on my ass."

Chance barked a laugh at the thought.

"Alright," he said through a chuckle. "Well, maybe we'll check back inside and see if Santa's Village has opened for business."

CHAPTER 19

On the way back inside, we cast our ballots for our favorite snow castles, and it took us a minute to remove all our layers of outerwear to readjust to the suffocating warmth of the interior.

Following the sounds of lively chatter, children playing, and more holiday music, the drawing room looked straight out of a movie. It was as if a movie set had been erected overnight, turning it into Santa's workshop. It was incredible.

I didn't think my mom had ever taken me to see Santa when I was little, but I remembered going once with my childhood best friend Jenny's family. But a mall Santa was a far cry from the childhood fantasy Chance and I had just walked into.

"Did your house look like this every year when you were a kid?" I asked Chance.

He let out a mirthless laugh. "No. I almost wonder if she's making up for the fact that our holidays weren't like this at all."

My brow furrowed. Chance had told me before about how holidays had been—I believe "perfunctory" was the word he had used—but I had a hard time reconciling that thought with what was laid out before me.

"Mom was running a company when Amanda and I were little, and Dad was building his empire. Holidays mostly consisted of being dragged along to the occasional society party that allowed for children. Sometimes they had a Santa there or a kids' area set up, I suppose. But it was mostly nannies and staff who did anything like a real holiday with us.

"I don't remember feeling particularly unhappy about it while growing up. It was all I knew, and yeah, it was different from what I saw in the movies, but I didn't think I was missing out on anything. It wasn't until I was in college at Oxford and got to spend the holidays with friends I had made there that I realized how much I'd missed out on. All these cozy, lovely family traditions, and just the warmth and love that you can palpably feel..."

Chance let out a long sigh. "My parents did their best, just like I'm sure your mom did. I always had a roof over my head and food in my stomach. So it feels shitty to complain."

I nodded in agreement. It still felt so weird that despite the chasm between the worlds in which we had grown up, there was still so much we shared...things I didn't wish we had in common. And at the very least, Cindy was trying so hard to make up for the time she'd lost with Chance when he had been younger. Even more, she was trying to create those core memories for other children, and ones who needed it. That had to count for something.

"The good news is that you and I get to make all our own memories and traditions, right?" I tried to cheer him up.

He smiled down at me. "Look at you turning into an optimist. I'm rubbing off on you, aren't I?"

I just shook my head. But he had. Of course he had.

"Not to be a downer, but I don't think we've got a shot at finding anything in here with all the backdrops up around the room, not to mention the gaggle of children." Chance was right, unfortunately.

"We could look through the other rooms and check those clocks, in case they got moved around to different spaces?" I threw out.

Chance grimaced. "Most everything else on the first floor is closed off, either with staff prep stations, or they're already setting things up for the masquerade ball."

"Guess we'll have to wait until tomorrow. Maybe we can find your mom after the festival closes later?" I suggested.

"It'll definitely be easier to find her after the event. We could go upstairs and get started on your holiday movie marathon early?" Chance posed.

I beamed at him. "Yes, please!"

But as we made our way through the hallway toward the grand staircase, we were waylaid.

"Chance. A word. In my office." Thomas Roberts blocked our path to freedom. Thomas, ever formidable, in an impeccably tailored suit, still intimidated me like no one else I'd ever encountered in my life. And I was sure, even if he wasn't Chance's father, I would have felt the same. It was simply the energy he exuded.

Chance looked down at me, an indecipherable expression upon his face. I wasn't sure if he was apologetic or desperate for me to argue that he couldn't go, so he had an excuse to leave with me.

Without waiting for Chance to agree, Thomas turned and walked back down the hallway to his study, assuming Chance would be right behind him.

"Ask him about the albums while you're in there," I reminded him. "He's your dad. It'll be fine. I'll wait for you upstairs."

With a frown marring his otherwise handsome visage, Chance turned and followed his father without uttering a single word, as if he were marching off to his own death.

CHAPTER 20

"Well? What did he want?" I called out to Chance the second he walked through the door to his bedroom.

He chuckled at my impatience. "Give me a minute." He slipped off his shoes and crossed the room, sliding into bed next to me, where I had been trying but failing to read a Euripides passage I wanted a refresh on before my spring semester lessons.

"What are you reading?" He tried to grab the book from me, but I held it just out of his reach.

"Now you're just trying to annoy me. Tell me what happened." I set the book down and turned to face him, tugging his hands into mine, between us.

"There were a few things." He turned on his side, mirroring me. "First, he wanted to know what Langston said about you at the fundraiser."

My eyebrows must have shot up to my hairline. "He did?"

"The second I finished relaying the story, he dialed him up, on speakerphone, and terminated his contract."

My lips parted in surprise. "Why would he do that?" I asked, my voice low. Of course I knew the answer, but that wasn't Thomas's

MO. He'd never shown any sort of affection or even consideration for me. I didn't even think he'd said my name before or acknowledged my presence more than just the occasional annoyed glare.

"He said he didn't care to employ people who disrespected his family."

"But I'm not..." I shook my head. Yes, I belonged to Chance, and I got along well with Amanda and Cindy, but I was his—I wasn't a part of their family. Did they think I was? Did they want me to be?

Chance's sharp blue-grey gaze softened. "Yes. You are."

I swallowed hard.

"He shouldn't have done that. Not for me."

My mind continued to whirl, trying to assign some sort of reason to his actions. Perhaps Cindy had convinced him to do so. But what if it was something else... What if Thomas was softening? What if, after everything he'd done, he was beginning to see the error of his ways?

I could only hope that might be the case, but I had to admit that him taking such swift and severe action with Langston, regardless of his motivations, felt like progress in some way. If there was the smallest possibility of Chance developing a better relationship with his father, as long as Thomas's motivations were pure, I felt like it would mean a lot to Chance, and perhaps even start healing long-open wounds that had developed as a result of their differences.

"It was the least he could have done," Chance asserted. "Langston is a piece of shit, and my dad is better off without his advice."

"He wasn't mad at how you reacted—that it was in front of everyone?" I'd been worried since the fundraiser that the way in which he'd defended me would come back to haunt us.

Chance shook his head against the pillow. "No. He didn't say anything. If he was mad, I think him knowing what was said would have changed his mind. If Langston had said something like that about my mom, in front of my dad..." Chance whistled through his teeth. "Langston would have had a broken nose and been knocked on his ass."

A soft laugh bubbled from my lips at the thought.

"But that was it? You were down there for a while." I'd been waiting for him for a couple hours.

Chance sighed. "No, that wasn't everything." He looked down at our hands, clasped between us. He was worried...Chance was rarely worried. That was my job.

"You can tell me. It's okay. As long as you still love me, I'll be okay," I said quietly.

Chance's eyes flitted to mine, filled with outrage. "Don't say shit like that," he admonished. "Of course I fucking love you. Don't ever question that. There is nothing my dad could say that would ever make me stop loving you."

"I'm sorry." I leaned forward, kissing him softly. "I'm sorry, Chance."

"He's demanding we sign a prenup," Chance confessed.

I sat up in the bed, but didn't sever our connection. "We're not even engaged."

We'd talked about marriage before, but it was always something that would happen someday. I wasn't in any rush because I didn't care if we were married, as long as we were together. Having a ring on my finger and a signed document wasn't going to change how I felt about Chance, so it just didn't really matter to me.

"He's just trying to get ahead of things. I think he's worried we'll elope or something."

Did Chance want to elope?

"Obviously I told him to fuck off." Chance tugged at my hands to get me to lie back down next to him.

"Why'd you do that?" I was confused.

"Because it's insulting that he'd expect that of you."

I released a strained laugh. "Don't be ridiculous—of course I'll sign a prenup."

"What!?" Chance gave up on getting me to lie back down and instead propped himself up. "Why?"

"Why?" I guffawed. "Because, financially, I bring nothing into a marriage, and your family is wealthy and has assets to protect."

"Protect from you? For the divorce we're going to go through?" Chance argued.

I huffed out a breath. "Chance..." I placed my hands on his cheeks to make sure he was looking me in the eyes. "Whenever we decide to get married, if we decide to get married at all—"

He chuffed.

"Of course I have no intention of getting a divorce," I continued, ignoring his outburst. "But I also have no interest in your family's money. This is an easy way to prove that to them and make sure they understand I am with you for you."

"But what if something happens to me—you could be left with nothing," he challenged.

"I can and will take care of myself. No matter what happens," I asserted. "What I won't do is have anyone question how much I care about you. I'll sign whatever he wants. None of it matters."

Chance pulled me into his arms, "You ridiculous, irrational, stubborn woman."

"If I've lost you, money would be my last concern," I whispered into his neck. "My heart would be too broken to care about anything else."

"Sweetheart..." He tightened his grip and I blinked back tears at the thought of a world without him in it. "I'm okay. I'm not going anywhere."

I nodded against him.

"Do you want to hear about the last thing we discussed?" he offered.

"How bad was it?" I mumbled into his chest.

"Good news, actually." Chance gently combed his fingers through my hair. "I asked him about the photo albums."

I looked up at Chance with hope. "And?"

"They're at an archival site so they don't deteriorate."

"You said it was good news." I pouted.

Chance's grin widened. "The archive digitized all the photos. Dad already emailed me the link."

"You could have led with that!" I shoved him playfully.

Thursday, December 23

CHAPTER 21

Roses. Roses everywhere.

My hope for finding the door was dwindling, and out of the two pieces, it was certainly the more important one. We could bust through a lock. But it would be much more difficult to find a hidden room if we couldn't find the entrance.

We'd spent the evening after the children's festival poring over all the digital photos we could find. It was easy to get lost in them; it was like stepping back through time. And what was even more vexing was seeing photographs of Mitzi and her actual husband, Alexander, Chance's grandfather, as their family grew. They seemed so happy together, and it made me all the more confused as to what had happened with Sasha.

Sure, it was easy to hide your emotions on the opposite side of a photographer's lens, but there were tons of candid shots, and I found it hard to believe that not a single one of them would have caught Mitzi in her feelings if she'd had a broken heart over Sasha. Maybe she had been the one to end things. It was difficult to reconcile the Mitzi from the letters, who was willing to sacrifice everything for Sasha, and the Sasha who was willing to walk away from her if it meant she'd be happy.

While we waited for the drawing room to clear out overnight, we were able to find a handful of photographs that had been taken in the drawing room, and there were several clocks we were able to spot in the sepia-toned images. These photographs would prove helpful if the clocks had been moved around in the house.

Chance insisted that his family had never, to his knowledge, auctioned anything off or gotten rid of any of the heirloom pieces in the house, especially not the decor, which Mitzi had felt very strongly about, which in turn, had made Cindy protective over the heirlooms.

We were able to sleep in again on Thursday morning, thankfully, and by the time we got downstairs, the house was one more abuzz with event workers setting up for the masquerade ball that evening.

"What even happens at a masquerade ball?" I asked Chance over coffee.

He laughed. "Mom's only thrown one before, a long time ago. From what I remember, it was just another regular gala except for the masks, which people take off at a designated time, to symbolize returning to reality from the fantasy of the ball."

I knew they had originated in Venice because the traditions were based on masked Roman festivities, something I noted in one of my classics lectures, but I hadn't given much thought as to what happened during one.

"Are we expected to become someone else while donning our masks?" I posed playfully.

"You can be whoever you want, muse." Chance leaned in to kiss the tip of my nose. "I'll still find you and make you mine."

"You two are insufferable," Amanda jokingly chimed as she walked into the kitchen.

"What time am I to report for duty?" I asked her, ignoring the innocent jab. She'd mentioned it would take a bit longer to get ready for the event this evening, but hadn't said why. And I was curious about the dress she'd picked. It hadn't been ready when I'd had the fitting with her on Saturday, so I had no idea what to expect, and she'd been teasing me all week about how stunning it was.

She looked down at her watch. "You've got about an hour."

"An hour!?" I choked.

"We need to redo your nails, and I want the makeup artist to do something a little special tonight so your eyes really pop under the mask," she replied nonchalantly as she helped herself to a cup of coffee.

"We better get over to the drawing room, then." Chance hopped off the barstool and took his dishes over to the sink to rinse them.

"What's in the drawing room?" Amanda asked curiously.

"Wouldn't you like to know?" Chance taunted.

Amanda scowled at him.

I shook my head, laughing under my breath as the siblings continued to squabble.

"My room. One hour!" Amanda called after me as I followed Chance out of the kitchen.

CHAPTER 22

"It's weird, but it looked different—bigger or something—in the old photos and even yesterday with all of the Santa's workshop stuff up," I commented to Chance as we entered the drawing room. It had been returned to normal after the children's festival, with brocade couches, elegantly carved wood tables in various shapes appointed throughout the room, artwork cluttering the walls, and all sorts of bric-a-brac scattered about.

"These event staff are like magicians," Chance chuckled.

Making my way over to the first clock I spotted, a neatly carved cuckoo clock hanging on the wall above a sideboard. With Mitzi's German heritage, I wasn't surprised to see the no doubt priceless antique. I'd remembered seeing the cuckoo clock in one of the old photos and had been drawn to it, thinking it would make a perfect place to hide a key.

I examined the clock, searching for...I wasn't sure, a secret compartment, or an obvious hiding spot for a key.

"I'm scared to touch it." I pointed to the clock.

Without another word, Chance came up next to me and plucked the clock from the wall.

"Chance!" I squawked.

"I'll touch the valuable or old stuff if you're worried about breaking anything, so if something happens, I can honestly say it was my fault," he explained, holding the clock gingerly and examining the different sides.

There was a latch on the back side, which he opened, showing the intricate inner workings of the clock and the mechanism that would allow for the bird to pop out on the hour, if programmed correctly.

"It's pretty solid," he told me, handing me the clock to take a look myself.

"Can you turn on your cell phone light?" I requested, thinking maybe the key was taped inside, since we couldn't hear anything rattling around as I gently tipped the clock in various directions.

Chance dutifully positioned the light at the angles I requested, until I was satisfied that the key likely wasn't inside. He gently closed the back latch and replaced the clock on the wall.

For the next hour, we followed the same procedure with the dozen or so clocks we found in the drawing room, of all shapes and sizes, some even hiding in plain sight, like the little ceramic chinoiserie cat figurine on one of the side tables that had a small clock embedded in the body of the animal. We'd almost missed that one.

But none of them seemed to be hiding a key.

"I need to go upstairs," I sighed in defeat.

"We can look again tomorrow with fresh eyes," Chance offered, slinging his arm around my shoulders. "And most of the event staff should be gone tomorrow, so we can look in some of the other rooms too."

"I really thought it'd be in here." I frowned as we made our way toward the grand staircase to find Amanda.

"If that key is still in this house, we will find it. I promise." Chance leaned in to kiss my temple.

I'd been speculating all week as to what my dress for the masquerade ball might look like. Amanda had been incredibly tight-lipped, not willing to offer even the slightest hint as to the design.

Seeing it in person, in all its glory, hanging in a clear garment bag across the room, I understood why she'd wanted to keep it a surprise.

It looked like it was made of starlight itself.

With delicate straps, a deep V neckline, and an A-line silhouette, I was sure that it would fit my petite frame perfectly. The dress was constructed of sequins and beading, masterfully stitched together to form one glittering gown. But beyond the sparkle, what really made the gown stand out was the coloring, which began as an ice blue at the top and slowly darkened to a deep midnight blue at the bottom hemline, with every shade of blue in between.

"Where did you find it?" I asked Amanda in awe as I examined the dress.

"I've got a lot of connections." She smiled, pleased with my reception.

"It's the most beautiful thing I think I've ever seen," I said with hushed reverence. "The blue shading matches Chance's eyes," I said more to myself.

"I thought you might think so." Amanda giggled.

"Will I be matching the theme downstairs again?" I quirked a brow at her.

Her grin widened. "You noticed that, huh?"

I returned her smile in acknowledgement.

"I thought it might help make you feel like you belonged, but also that you could sort of blend in, if you needed to..." she offered.

Her thoughtfulness continued to warm me. "Thank you." I reached out, squeezing her hand. "You have no idea how much your kindness means to me."

"You're my sister," she said softly. "I'll always take care of my family."

Her words rendered me speechless. I gave her a tight nod, blinking back tears. Having grown up an only child, and as someone who had never made friends easily, she would never know how deeply I cherished the gift she had given me in her friendship, let alone a sisterhood.

We spent the next few hours undergoing various makeup, hair, and beauty treatments to prepare for the event, chattering with ease about her plans in California and the various goings on at Montgomery.

When it came time for me to put the dress on, I was surprised at the weight of it. Every step I took that evening, I would be fully aware of the beautiful garment. Because of the sparkle the dress offered, Amanda kept my jewelry simple with just the necklace Chance had given me and the same modest pair of dainty dangling earrings I'd worn the night of the auction.

"I feel like a princess," I'd told Amanda as she fastened me into the dress.

"Would you like a tiara?" she asked with all seriousness.

"No!" I blurted.

Amanda practically cackled in response.

I watched her in the mirror as she placed a soft black lace mask over my face, tying the satin ribbon neatly at the back of my head. She told me all the women would be wearing similar black lace masks they'd be given at the door, while the men had solid fabric versions.

Amanda's hair stylist had fashioned my hair into gentle waves, rather than an updo for the ball, and although I hated to admit it, the brown smokey eyeshadow her makeup artist had provided, complete with wispy false lashes and gentle black winged eyeliner, made my eyes look phenomenal even through the lace mask.

"You've really outdone yourself, Amanda," I told her, admiring the entire ensemble in the mirror. "Thank you again for all the time and effort you've put into making me look beautiful and feel comfortable this week."

Amanda rested her elbow on my shoulder, admiring her handi-work as well. "The pleasure was all mine, Violet." She beamed. "I told you, I always wanted a sister I could play dress-up with, and now I have one."

I could only smile in return, blinking back happy tears, not want-ing to ruin my makeup before the party had even begun.

"Shall we?" She extended her elbow, allowing me to hook my arm through hers.

Linked, we walked through the hallway and down the grand staircase, observing as guests entered, fastening their masks on after checking their coats, and making their way into the ballroom where the party was well underway, with food, drink, live music, and per-formers throughout the space.

As promised, my dress was perfectly on theme, coordinat-ing spectacularly with the brilliant shades of blue and sparkling snowflakes dripping from the vaulted ceiling of the grand entrance hall and likely continuing into the ballroom. Once again, the Christ-mas trees in the room had been redecorated with blue, white, and silver ornaments of all shapes and sizes.

Halfway down the stairs, I spotted Chance in a navy blue tuxedo that made him look nothing if not swoon-worthy. And of course, the color of his suit would match my dress magnificently. The black fabric mask he wore only managed to make his blue-grey eyes that much more striking.

"Have you seen my girlfriend?" Chance asked when he met us at the bottom of the stairs. "Gorgeous, brunette, sassy as hell, and yea high." He held his hand at his waist, to which I scowled. "Oh, it's you!" he joked. "I'd recognize that look anywhere."

"I hate you," I teased, taking his hand.

"I love you." He leaned down to give me a soft kiss on the lips. "Give me a twirl," he requested, stepping back from me.

I felt my cheeks heat, but gave him a brief spin nonetheless.

"Absolutely ravishing," he whispered in my ear, his tone heated.

"You're quite devastating yourself, sir." I tugged on his lapel.

"I might need you to call me sir more often." He raised a brow suggestively.

"Chance..." I warned.

"I look like a superhero reject," he chuckled. "But I'll take devastating all day long, especially if it's coming from you."

"You're a terrible flirt," I chided, not bothering to hide my smile.

Unable to help himself, Chance leaned down to kiss me again, his lips lingering against mine a bit longer than the first time.

"Gross." Amanda rolled her eyes. "Have you seen Hiram?"

"Grabbing you a drink from the bar," Chance replied, without missing a beat.

"Have fun, you two." Amanda gave me a small wave before disappearing into the masked crowd.

"Now what?" I asked Chance.

"Now we go find a dark corner to occupy for the rest of the evening, so I can take advantage of you."

"Can I eat something first?" I ignored the implication behind his suggestive words.

"If you insist."

CHAPTER 23

After less than two hours, Chance and I were bored with the ball. Content to hang around in the shadows and observe the other guests, there wasn't much else for us to do, considering we didn't want to dance in front of everyone, and we'd already had our fill of champagne and hors d'oeuvres.

"Wanna sneak back upstairs and have sex?" Chance whispered in my ear.

My eyes shot open, a nervous giggle escaping my lips. We were tucked away in a corner, but still surrounded by people.

"I'll take that as a yes." He laughed with me. "The stage is blocking the easiest route to the back stairs, so we'll have to take the long way around to avoid getting caught."

"Lead the way, Romeo," I joked.

Slowly, we began to edge our way around the ballroom. After about twenty minutes, we were about halfway down the hallway when I spotted his father exiting his study, and pulled Chance into the closest door.

We tumbled into the music room, another palatial space, with a gorgeous grand piano situated in the corner and room for plenty of tables or chairs, should Cindy wish to host a small concert in the room.

"Can't wait until we're upstairs?" Chance waggled his eyebrows at me.

"No." I swiped at him. "Didn't you see your dad? We would have run right into him. Just give it a minute and we'll see if the coast is clear."

"We could just lock the doors," Chance suggested.

I cocked my head. "Nice try." I stuck my tongue out at him, making my way over toward the piano. "Come play something for me." I beckoned Chance, recalling that he used to mess around on the out-of-tune piano up in the lounge from time to time.

"Only if you sit on my lap," he demanded, grabbing my hand and dragging me over to the piano bench.

"Careful," I warned him as he tried to grab me. The dress was so heavy and fragile, I didn't want to hurt it.

He raised his hands in the air, and allowed me to gently seat myself on his thigh, before wrapping his arms around me to reach the keys and beginning to play the soft notes of "Clair de lune." "This one was always Mom's favorite," he told me, his hands dancing gracefully as they stroked each key, his knee moving beneath me to utilize the pedals as needed.

"I always preferred *Moonlight Sonata*—moody little shit that I was," he chuckled, seamlessly changing to the darker melody.

I was in awe of him.

"What about you?" he asked.

I laughed against him. "I'm more of a 'Bohemian Rhapsody' girl, myself."

Without skipping a beat, he began to play the ballad portion of the song. I felt my smile widen.

"You should sing along," he told me.

"No way." I shook my head. "I'm practically tone deaf."

"I know." His melodic laughter rang in my ears. "I can hear you singing in the shower sometimes."

We both had a good chuckle at that thought.

"How about this one?" He changed tunes again.

I knew it was a pop song, but it took me a moment to remember the title. "'Tiny Dancer'!" I shouted out.

I could feel him grinning against my temple, his fingers eventually falling away from the piano as his hands trailed up my arms while I turned to face him. Gently, he traced his fingers along my jaw before he pulled me into him, kissing me softly, yet so soundly.

"I'm glad you came with me this week," he said against my mouth.

"Me too..." I murmured.

And when he kissed me again, the undertone transformed into something much more heated than before. His tongue slid into my mouth, commanding me to surrender with every stroke. When I managed to disentangle myself from him, we were panting for breath.

"How long is it going to take to get you out of that dress?" His voice was low and husky, his eyes darkened with desire in the dim lighting of the music room.

"Not long, if you ask nicely," I purred, leaning into him.

"I'll drag you upstairs even if the coast isn't clear," he threatened.

"Deal," I demurred, gently rising from his lap and stepping back from the piano bench toward the front wall, lined with two huge arched sash windows. Then I did a double-take.

"Did they add a wall to this room?" I asked Chance suddenly, walking toward the wall in question to examine it more closely.

"What? No. Why?" He followed me in confusion.

"The photos—the music room had four windows—it was a corner room." I looked around the room, and then it hit me: "They swapped the rooms..." I muttered.

"What?" Chance was still catching up.

"I think this used to be the drawing room. It's right off the entrance hall, which would have made sense back then—easier access for guests. Your family doesn't even use the current drawing room except for events, but Amanda told me your mom hosts concerts for her charity a few times a year." I stormed across the floor to the first clock I saw, on the mantel.

"They switched the room..." Chance repeated, realizing what I was suggesting.

I plucked the mantel clock off the shelf, and when I went to turn it over, something metal made a clinking noise inside. My heart stuttered.

Carefully, I unlatched the back and tipped the clock. A brass key clattered to the floor.

Chance's eyes went wide. "No fucking way," he breathed.

"Now we just need to find the door." I grinned up at him victoriously.

FRIDAY,
DECEMBER 24

CHAPTER 24

I smelled coffee.

That was the first thought I had as I stirred awake the next morning.

Chance's room was bathed in light, telling me I'd been allowed to sleep in again. And there was no better day than Christmas Eve to sleep in. After all, it was the first thing to check off my Christmas Eve tradition to-do list.

There was a soft shuffling beside me. I turned, squinting, and saw Chance in a deep red sweater—how festive—setting a tray on his nightstand.

"Morning, baby." He leaned over his side of the bed and kissed my forehead.

This man was going to be the end of me.

"What time is it?" I rubbed my eyes as I sat up in bed.

"Almost ten, but we were up late..."

I glanced over to the foot of the bed where I'd left my gown the night before in a heap on the floor, right in the spot where Chance had removed it before we'd finished the evening in bed.

"I regret nothing." I smirked.

Chance chuckled, reaching out to hand me a steaming mug of coffee.

"Thank you," I murmured, meeting his blue-grey gaze, still smiling. I looked behind him at the tray, and my eyes widened. "Are those chocolate croissants!?"

"Wouldn't be Christmas Eve without them." He beamed, pulling the tray between us on the bed and carefully getting back into bed.

"You remembered..."

"Of course I did, especially after our disastrous trial run last year."

And, thankfully, we weren't snowed in again with only vending machine food to sustain us. Although it was because of that disastrous Christmas Eve that we'd taken the next step in our relationship. I found that maybe I didn't mind so much that things hadn't gone to plan.

"When you're done eating, we're going downstairs and hunting for hummingbirds," he informed me. With what had better be Mitzi's key in hand, I was more determined than ever to find that stupid door.

I glanced up at Chance, who was watching me with gleaming eyes.

"You're acting suspicious." I pointed a butter knife at him.

He reached out and lowered the knife. "I thought we were past you threatening me with knives, Violet, darling," he joked.

I rolled my eyes and set the knife back on the tray. "Why are you being so nice?"

He huffed a laugh. "I'm not allowed to be nice to you?"

I frowned, narrowing my eyes. Something was up, but I couldn't put my finger on it.

"C'mon, finish eating. We've got, what…" He glanced at his wristwatch. "Five, six hours before Amanda grabs you to get ready for dinner. And we're leaving right after presents tomorrow morning, so this might be our last chance to look."

He made a good point. I inwardly groaned at the idea of the last revelry event we'd be attending, an exclusive donor's dinner. Lord knows who we'd get stuck next to this time.

"I'm going, I'm going," I puffed before taking a hurried sip of my coffee, then a giant bite of croissant.

Knowing we'd be traipsing around the house all day, I threw on the same comfortable jeans and riding boots I'd worn for the children's festival and found an oversized, chunky, forest green cable-knit turtleneck sweater that Amanda had set out, along with a few other sweater options for the duration of my stay.

Feeling a little festive, I pulled a red velvet ribbon off a box and used it to tie up half of my hair.

Chance and I spent the entirety of the afternoon going through each room systematically, noting all the versions of hummingbirds we found and exploring around the area where they were located to see if there was any indication of some hidden seam in the wall, loose floorboards, or something else entirely.

While we stopped searching temporarily for lunch, I used my phone to research common places for people to hide hidden doorways in the early eighteen hundreds, when the house had been originally built.

"Google says they were most commonly built behind fireplaces, bookshelves—SEE I TOLD YOU"—I glared at Chance, whose shoulders shook with silent laughter at my outburst—"under staircases, or behind large paintings or tapestries."

"There's quite a few large paintings, and some of them had hummingbirds," he offered.

"Maybe we should focus on these suggestions and see if we can find hummingbirds around them, instead of starting with the hummingbirds?" I suggested.

"We've got nothing to lose at this point." He stabbed at his salad.

But by the time the sky was darkening, with evening approaching, none of those options had panned out.

"I need to go upstairs and find Amanda to get ready for dinner," I sulked. "Would your mom be mad if I pretended to be sick?" I looked up at Chance. "I don't know if I can stand another few hours listening to these old men complaining about the most inane point zero zero zero one percent problems."

Chance reached out, tucking my hair behind my ear. "It'll be okay. I'll be there with you."

I pursed my lips and glanced over his shoulder at the grand staircase. "I should go..."

"Can I show you something quick?" Chance asked.

My brow furrowed.

"Amanda won't mind waiting."

"What is it?" I asked, narrowing my eyes with suspicion.

Chance just laughed, grabbing my hand. "It'll only take a second. It's in the atrium."

Nervously, I followed him as we made our way down the hall toward the glass room that was definitely my favorite place in Harper House.

Before we even got to the atrium, I could see the illumination from the warm lights strung up inside, pouring out into the hallway. But nothing could have prepared me for what was inside.

Half of the floor had been cleared to make room for a large palette of blankets and pillows. A large low tray held steaming bowls of mac and cheese, with a silver ice bucket cradling a bottle of sparkling cider, two pristine champagne flutes sitting neatly next to it.

The pièce de résistance was a large screen affixed to the wall of windows in front of the bedding, across from a projector hidden behind some greenery at the back of the room. The credits to *Home Alone* were already playing, with the infamous tinkling of the movie's score filtering through speakers I couldn't locate.

"When we're ready, there's hot chocolate and cheesecake for dessert." He squeezed my hand. "I don't think it's supposed to snow tonight, but the stars are out, so hopefully the view in here will suffice."

"Chance..." I turned to him, tears welling in my eyes.

"Merry Christmas, Violet," he replied softly, his eyes twinkling with mirth.

I launched myself into his arms, kissing him fiercely, showing him the best way I knew how, how appreciative I was of what he'd done.

He laughed against me at my ferocity, but I couldn't get enough of him.

Reluctantly, needing to catch my breath, I pulled away, my lips swollen and my cheeks heated. I rested my head against Chance's forehead. "I am so thankful, every damn day, that you didn't give up on me last year," I whispered.

"I'll never give up on you, sweetheart." He smiled.

CHAPTER 25

This was easily the best Christmas Eve I'd ever had, hands down. I didn't think it would even be possible to top it.

For hours, Chance and I cuddled in our blanket pile, gorging on mac and cheese and cheesecake, giggling at the holiday movies that I used to watch to feel something, to know what it was like for people who grew up with big families and annoying siblings. It was a way for me to relive a childhood that I'd never really had because of my mother's depression. It wasn't her fault, but that time was simply gone.

"Can I tell you a secret?" I whispered to Chance.

He looked down at me where I was nestled against his shoulder. "Always."

I bit my lip, debating on if I really wanted to share my thoughts with him. But I decided I trusted he wouldn't use it against me. "I think...I think I might like surprises, when they're from you."

Chance huffed a laugh, his chest rumbling with the sound of his amusement. "Awfully brave of you to admit it," he teased.

"Yeah, well, don't do anything unreasonable," I warned, readjusting in his hold.

Staring up at the domed ceiling overhead, beyond which the stars trembled and flickered, I wanted to soak in every single moment of this evening. I had the distinct sense it would be one of those memories I would want to revisit often, so the more detail, the better.

And it was while I was looking through to the heavens that my eye caught on the apex of the metal framework of the domed atrium. I sat up suddenly, squinting at the ridges on the patinated bronze circle that formed the apex, because there was a design on it.

"What's wrong?" Chance sat up next to me, following my gaze to the ceiling. "Did you see a shooting star?"

"Where's my phone?" I patted my hand amongst the blankets until I found it, turning on the flashlight and shining it overhead, revealing the outline of a hummingbird stamped in the metal.

Mouth agape, I looked down at Chance, who was staring back at me with wide eyes.

"You don't think…" he trailed off.

"The letters said 'beneath the hummingbird'—multiple times," I reiterated as I began to scan the room. We were slightly off center due to a tree in a large planter that sat in the middle of the room. "You'd have a perfect view of the rose gardens from the atrium, and it could explain why Mitzi stowed the letters in here."

Scrambling off the blankets, I grabbed for the riding boots, tugging them on quickly, then used my phone to examine the space around the tree, circling it. "It probably wasn't even here a hundred years ago." I glanced up at Chance, who was watching me with keen interest.

The tiles beneath it looked to be a slightly darker color, but that could have easily been explained by dirt from the planter...unless they were discolored for a different reason. "Help me move the planter." I motioned Chance over, who was lacing up his shoes.

It took us a few minutes to slide the planter far enough that the tiles beneath were completely exposed, revealing an almost invisible ring pull that sat flush against the tiles. Upon further examination, there was definitely a seal around the four large square tiles that sat beneath the planter. "It's a hatch!" I told Chance.

"Maybe we should go get help..." Chance swallowed hard, nervous as to what we might find below. After the gruesome discovery we'd made in the attic of the carriage house the year before, I didn't blame him, but we had no reason to believe anything nefarious was lurking within.

"No way!" I squatted down, tugging at the ring pull. The hatch moved a tiny bit, which meant it wasn't locked, but it was too heavy for me to open. "Help me, please," I pleaded with Chance.

He glanced at the doorway, but it was late. The staff was likely gone and his family would be asleep upstairs. "It could be dangerous..."

"We'll be careful," I told him in a rush, the excitement of our discovery too overwhelming to turn back now. "We'll stop if it's not safe."

Chance pursed his lips. "Promise?"

He knew I wasn't going to give up, but giving into this one demand was reasonable. "Promise," I stated firmly.

He exhaled a loud sigh, still wary, but stepped forward to try the hatch anyway. "Back up a little, just in case the ground isn't solid," he instructed.

I took two steps back just to ease his mind, but I wasn't worried.

Bracing his legs, he used his body weight as leverage and heaved the hatch door open with a grunt, almost falling back with the effort, but able to catch his footing at the last moment.

We scrambled around the door to find a set of stone stairs leading down into a maw of solid darkness.

"We should come back in the morning...when it's light out." Chance was tense, staring into the void.

"Please..." I grabbed his arm. "I won't be able to sleep. I just want to try. We're right here."

Chance's shoulders slumped. We both knew he was going to give in. "Fine." He huffed another begrudging sigh. "But I'm going down first. And if we hear anything, we're coming right back up and closing it, no arguments."

"No arguments," I repeated, nodding my head in agreement.

Chance looked around the atrium and paced over to a corner to grab a broom before returning to my side.

I looked at it questioningly.

"I can see cobwebs, and if someone's down there, I could use it as a weapon," he reasoned.

I pursed my lips, stifling a laugh. With the amount of dust and cobwebs we could see up at the top, I highly doubted anyone would be down there.

"You have the key?" he asked.

I nodded, sticking my hand in my pocket and running my fingers along the ridges of the warm brass key. I hadn't wanted to leave it in the room, afraid that after searching for so long that it would vanish without a trace.

"Keep your light up to help me see, okay?" He looked back at me.

"I will." I held it up, smiling at him encouragingly.

With achingly slow steps, we made our way down the stone stairs. Chance used the broom to clear away the abandoned detritus overhead and tested each step for stability before allowing me to follow. The stairs gently curved around, and once we were a little more than halfway down, we saw a door at the base.

Chance took a few deep breaths, steadying himself before he asked me for the key, which fit into the lock perfectly, the tumblers inside clicking as they disengaged. I aimed the light at the handle, which Chance tentatively reached toward, wrapping his hand around the dusty, but ornately designed round doorknob, and turned it.

The door creaked, dust swirling around us as it was dislodged with the movement.

He pushed the door open, still standing on the stairs' side of the threshold. The door swung inward, thumping against the interior wall a moment later. I angled the flashlight through the gap, illuminating the room for the first time in decades.

On the right side of the small room was a well-worn leather Chesterfield couch and a coffee table. Opposite that was a small writing desk, strewn with letters. A thick layer of dust coated everything, but the room was in better shape than the hallway, the door having protected the space from more of the grit.

Chance's posture visibly relaxed when it became clear that the room was empty. Taking his hand, I marched past him toward the writing desk, nudging the matching bench to the side slightly so I could stand right before it.

On the desk was another leather portfolio, with an even thicker stack of letters tucked inside. A cursory glance revealed them to be more love letters between Mitzi and Sasha. My heart soared at the thought of finding out more of their story.

Chance pulled open one of the desk drawers, which held a few old pens, but also a journal. He picked it up to tab through the pages, and as he did, something slipped from between them and fell to the floor.

I bent down to pick it up, shining my light on it. It was a photograph, albeit a very old one. I immediately recognized Mitzi from the photo albums we'd gone through.

"That's my grandfather." Chance pointed to the young man she had her arms wrapped around.

I turned it over, and on the back, in Mitzi's signature cursive, it was labeled "Mitzi & Sasha (1945)."

I flipped the dusty and aged photo back over. "You're sure?" I examined the man again, but Chance was right. That was his grandfather. We'd seen countless photos of them together in the digital files we'd searched through. "But it says 'Sasha.'" I turned the photo over again, showing the label to Chance.

His lips began to curl into a smile. "Sasha's my grandfather..."

I felt tears welling in my eyes at the thought. Since we'd first realized what the letters had been, I'd been preparing myself to experience their heartbreak. How could a woman of her station be allowed to marry a man who was considered to be of a lesser class? I'd been certain their story wouldn't end well, however, I'd been determined to know for sure.

But they'd lived a long and happy life together, raising a beautiful family. I wiped away the tears that had fallen down my cheeks, overcome with emotion. "They got to be together..." I whispered to Chance.

He wrapped an arm around me, pulling me into a tight, warm embrace.

SATURDAY,
DECEMBER 25

CHAPTER 26

Knowing that I would get to sleep in my own bed that night was the only thing propelling me through the following morning.

Chance and I had stayed up until the early hours of the morning poring over the new letters we'd discovered in Mitzi and Sasha's secret room beneath the atrium.

Through the letters, we learned that Mitzi had hatched a plan to invent a public persona for Sasha so he would be accepted by their social circles. In true Mitzi fashion, the story was outlandish, claiming that Sasha's family was of Russian noble lineage and had fled during the Bolshevik revolution, which would require him to adopt her surname of Harper when they married, to retain his anonymity. She'd used the scheme to convince her parents to allow for their union, and it had worked.

Reading through more of their love story made me ache for them, but eased the tension that had been building internally for days.

Absently touching the necklace Chance had given me made me feel even more connected to Mitzi and Sasha. I loved feeling like I had a piece of their history with me, and maybe their love story would continue, in a way, through me and Chance.

While putting on one last outfit chosen by Amanda, another cashmere sweater, this one in cream, wide-leg trousers in a deep burgundy, and camel-colored ankle booties that made me look much taller than I really was, I listened to Chance prattle on about how he thought maybe a local historical society or museum might be interested in the letters and how he'd love to work on a mixed media exhibit to showcase their family history and share Mitzi and Sasha's story with the world.

My heart felt so full hearing how excited he was about his idea. I vowed to do whatever I could to help him make it a reality. He'd also been buzzing since we'd decided the night before to share our discovery with his mom, who he knew would love to read about her parents' love story, and how hard they'd fought to be together.

Downstairs, Chance's family had gathered in the cozier morning room to share a casual breakfast and exchange presents. I savored the first sip of my coffee as I watched Cindy dole out presents to everyone. My eyes widened as she placed the last one on the coffee table in front of me.

"It's from Santa." She patted my hand in an attempt to reassure me.

Thomas went first, his face softening as he found a pair of antique cuff links nestled inside a small velvet box. Seeing the rare emotion on his face made me think they must have been sentimental. "Thank you, honey." He clasped Cindy's hand, squeezing it tenderly, like Chance often did with me.

For all his bravado, Thomas clearly adored his wife. Perhaps it was her who had managed to encourage him to soften toward Chance and me. Cindy had a kind heart, and I wanted to believe that if she loved Thomas so dearly, there might be a speck of a redeeming quality in the formidable magnate.

Next was Amanda, who squealed with delight when she unwrapped the large flat parcel to find a vintage watercolor painting of Harper House, showcasing the rose bushes that dotted the front lawn. "So you'll always have home with you," Cindy offered. "I know you've always loved that painting."

She set the painting down and launched herself at her mom, hugging her tightly. My heart hurt watching them together. I wished that I could have had that kind of relationship with my mom. But it had to be enough that she was happy back in Michigan with her found family.

Hiram's gift seemed heavy as he cautiously unwrapped the box to find a bottle of whiskey that looked to be very old. He grinned up, not at Cindy, but at Thomas. "Excellent vintage, sir."

"From my personal collection," Thomas replied curtly.

"Thank you." Hiram beamed at Thomas.

It seemed the two of them had mended the rift formed during the disastrous family dinner on Sunday night when Amanda had announced her impending departure. If the knowing grin on Cindy's face was any indication, the clever matriarch had indeed had something to do with Thomas's defrosting.

Chance was next in line, and his eyes lit up when the first swipe at the wrapping paper revealed the DSLR camera model I'd told Cindy he'd had his eye on. He smiled at me first, before turning his attention to his mom. "Thanks, Santa." He gave her a cheeky wink.

She shook her head, holding back laughter.

And then all eyes swung to me. The perfectly wrapped gift was small, thin, and rectangular. I thought perhaps it might be a journal, given the size and shape, and the fact that I had simple tastes and wanted for nothing.

Ignoring my nerves at the attention I was receiving, I gently tore back the paper and slid out the thin box that wasn't a journal. I turned it over.

"It's an e-reader, dear," Cindy told me.

My gaze met hers. I'd wanted one for forever, but it had always felt like an unnecessary expense while I was still trying to pay off my student loans and keep up with bills.

"I saw Chance lugging all those books up to your room on Sunday, and I thought this might make things easier for when you travel." She smiled warmly.

"Thank you." I looked down at the device, then back up at Cindy. "This is incredibly thoughtful."

"I snuck a gift card inside so you can load it up with whatever books you want." She grinned. "I might recommend Jackie Collins—she's one of my favorites."

"TMI, mom," Amanda groaned, as the author was known for her particularly salacious romance novels.

"She's going to keep me up all night reading in bed with that thing," Chance carped.

"Oh hush." Cindy waved a hand at him.

While the family moved on to some additional gifts, I took the opportunity to give Chance his surprise. I was so excited to see him open up the handmade ornament I'd found at the charity market-place.

"It looks just like the lounge!" He grinned, leaning in to give me a peck on the lips. "I love it!"

He then reached behind him and procured a tiny bag, passing it to me with a sheepish expression on his face, because it was the bag from the jeweler.

"You're an awful liar." I shook my head, reaching into the bag to pull out the small velvet box with the gleaming pair of diamond studs he'd chosen.

"I told you to get at least a carat," Amanda ribbed him from across the room.

"Violet prefers to be more discreet, so I picked a smaller size." He admonished her as I slipped out my cheap earrings, replacing them with the new ones. It did make my heart flutter to hear him not only defend me, but also that he'd remembered and understood my preferences.

"When are you all heading out?" Cindy asked, and there was a somber note to her voice.

"Not until you've gotten your present." Chance smiled broadly, pulling out the stack of letters he'd hidden behind the couch when we'd arrived.

Cindy's brow furrowed. "What are those?"

"Mitzi and Sasha's love letters," Chance told her.

Cindy's face immediately crumpled, tears welling in her eyes.

"Who's Sasha?" Amanda asked, brow furrowed.

"My dad." Cindy's voice cracked, her emotions coming through.

"Grandpa's name was Alexander." Amanda was still confused.

"Sasha is a Russian nickname for Alexander. Dad's descended from a line of Russian nobles, remember?" Cindy explained to Amanda as she crossed the room, kneeling in front of Chance and me.

"I'm not so sure about that..." Chance said as we shared a knowing look, although I was confident Cindy would find Mitzi's concocted story just as brilliant as we did.

"These are priceless." She glanced up at us. "Where on earth did you find them?"

Chance's smile widened. "In the secret room hidden under the atrium," he said with no fanfare.

Immediately his family erupted, one talking over the other, demanding details, shocked at the discovery, wanting to know how we'd found it.

"I'll show you," Chance offered, standing from the couch. He extended his hand to me, but I shook my head.

"You all go ahead. I'm going to go upstairs and pack...maybe call my mom. This is something you should do with your family."

"You sure?" I knew he wanted to argue that I belonged with them, and perhaps I did, but I was still exhausted, and having a moment alone sounded exactly like what I needed.

I nodded. Chance kissed my cheek, then motioned for his family to follow him.

I watched as they all filed out of the room toward the atrium, taking one last sip of coffee before heading back upstairs.

CHAPTER 27

One by one, I replaced each of the gorgeous dresses I'd been able to borrow back into their garment bags and hung them on the rack that Amanda had wheeled in nearly a week ago when I'd arrived. The blue, shimmering masquerade ball dress was easily my favorite. Just like the night before in the atrium, I had a feeling I'd be replaying my piano lesson with Chance on repeat for a long time.

How was it possible that in such a short amount of time, despite the rough start at the beginning of the week, I felt somewhat transformed? I'd walked into this house unsure of my place, and now felt as though I was leaving, having solidified that I belonged among the Harpers for better or worse.

While cleaning up, I made a quick call to my mother to wish her a merry Christmas. Like most years, she seemed appreciative of the gesture, but was distracted by Jake and Jenny's children, as they shared Christmas with her, having adopted her as part of their family, and leaving me to make my own, I supposed.

Chance joined me while I was finishing folding the sweaters, pants, and other more casual items that Amanda had curated for me on top of his dresser. "Amanda said those are yours now." He slipped his hand around my waist, pulling my back to his front. "Her Christmas presents to you."

"But I didn't get anything for her..." I pouted.

"She thought you'd say that and said you can come visit her in California in return."

"That sounds like another gift for me, not for her..." I frowned, folding the last sweater and placing it on top of the pile.

"She told me those jeans were a gift for me too because of how great your ass looks in them." He nipped at my ear.

"You're ridiculous—she did not say that." I couldn't help but laugh. "What did your family think of the room?" I turned around, looping my arms over his shoulders.

"Mom was in absolute awe. She said Grandma used to disappear for a couple hours some days, after her dad died, when she was younger, and she always wondered where she went, and now she knows." He leaned forward, kissing the tip of my nose. "I think it brought her a lot of peace to have this last surprise from her mother, and to have found it before leaving the house means a lot."

"I'm so glad we didn't give up." I smiled up at him.

"Told you, muse, never giving up on you and your stubborn, but fantastic, ass." He grinned at my annoyed expression, giving me another peck on the lips before retreating into the closet to begin packing his things.

Working together, and with an extra suitcase that miraculously, albeit suspiciously, appeared in order to hold the new clothes Amanda had gifted me, things went quite a bit faster. While I was looking forward to a quiet dinner, just the two of us, in our apartment, I found that I was feeling a bit melancholy at the thought of leaving.

"Want to say goodbye to the room before we hit the road?" Chance asked, after lugging the suitcases downstairs.

I smiled up at him; he knew me so well.

Slipping my hand in Chance's, we made our way toward the atrium at the back of the house.

"I can't tell you how relieved I was when we realized that Sasha was really my grandfather," Chance told me. "Even though he died before I was born, she told me so many stories about all their adventures. He loved how much of a troublemaker she was."

We laughed together at the thought. And having read their letters, I believed it. It was clear there was just as much laughter in their relationship as there was love. Just like me and Chance.

The hatch was still propped open when we entered the atrium. The stone stairwell didn't look nearly as foreboding in the daylight, but as it curved around the corner, Chance still needed to turn on his phone's flashlight to help us see as we descended, hand in hand.

"She always told me how he was the love of her life—her soulmate," Chance continued. "And that always made me happy knowing that kind of love was out in the world, and that I might get to experience a love like theirs one day." He squeezed my hand.

I swallowed the lump in my throat. He was being so sweet. Then again, Chance was always sweet with me.

"And now I *do* know." He turned slightly to look at me, just as we made it to the bottom of the stairs. "Because I've found the love of my life, too."

I blinked back tears as I looked up at him. "I love you, too," I whispered as he pushed open the door.

He moved to the side, allowing me to enter the room before him, shining his light over toward the desk. "That's weird; what's that?"

I turned to look at the desk to find his light was fixed on an open jewelry box, a delicate gold ring nestled inside.

I spun around to find Chance down on one knee, my hands flew over my mouth in shock.

"Every moment without you is a moment wasted, Violet," he told me. "I don't ever want to be without you. Marry me."

I crumpled to the floor, hugging him, completely overwhelmed but never happier in my life, as I sobbed a "yes" into his chest, the ring forgotten behind me.

FRIDAY, DECEMBER 31

EPILOGUE

"Ta da!" Amanda waved her hands with a flourish as she unveiled the dress she'd picked for me for the New Year's Eve gala.

Even I'd admit I had to pick my jaw up off the ground. It was everything.

The black dress had long sleeves, another deep V-neck—Amanda insisted that was best to elongate my petite figure—a full skirt, with a slit up one side, and was belted at the waist, which made the dress feel modern and sleek, especially combined with the slit. But my favorite part was the shoulders, which were embellished with crystal, silver, and gold beading in a floral and geometric pattern.

"It looks like armor," I commented, running the tip of my finger over the intricate beadwork.

"I thought so too," Amanda gushed.

"How far up does the slit go?" I bent down to examine the cut of the fabric.

"Mid-thigh, but the skirt is so full, you won't notice it, and I promise it won't cause a scandal," she replied expertly, likely having anticipated that I might mention having concerns.

"And the shoes?" I raised a brow, staring at the black, strappy heels.

"Thick heels and cushioned insoles; you'd be surprised how comfortable they are." She folded her arms over her chest, waiting for more issues to rebuke.

I cracked a smile; she'd done such a good job picking out something that felt like so much of me. "It's really pretty." I ran my hand over the thick fabric that looked and felt like a matte satin.

"And it'll go perfect with your ring!" Amanda exclaimed, looking down at my hand, where the elegant little piece of jewelry sat, as if it had always belonged there.

In the center of the gold ring was a square-cut alexandrite gemstone that was mounted at a forty-five-degree angle, so it was in the orientation of a diamond. Along each side of the center stone were small filigree leaves with tiny diamonds embedded in between the metalwork.

Cindy had given it to Chance for the proposal, it having belonged to Mitzi before me. It was Victorian in origin, and Mitzi had claimed that it was the ring Sasha had proposed with. Per two minutes of searching online, I learned that alexandrite had been discovered in Russia in the early eighteen hundreds and quickly became a symbol of status for Russian royalty, nobles, and elites.

While Mitzi had likely procured the ring separately and then used it as further evidence to Sasha's claim of noble heritage, the fact that my engagement ring was another lovely reminder of the letters and secret room we'd discovered, as well as of Mitzi and Sasha's epic love, made me adore it even more.

Funnily enough, Chance told me he'd only chosen it because he'd liked that the stone, which shifted colors in different lighting, often appearing violet. He'd mentioned this with a smirk, before explaining that he'd been drawn to the color-shifting properties because he felt like it represented my resilience. I'd never swooned harder in my life.

The truth was, I couldn't have even dreamt up a more perfect ring. The smaller size suited me perfectly, as it wasn't ostentatious, but was still unique. I loved everything about it, really, including the history, but especially that he had picked it just for me.

"I'm still surprised that he got one over on you," Amanda commented. "He was so obvious when he asked to talk to Mom after dinner last week. I thought for sure you'd catch on."

My brow furrowed. "That's when he got the ring?"

Amanda nodded.

And then a cascade of pieces fell into place. Cindy had commented about how the trip to Greece Chance had won during the silent auction would be a good honeymoon, and I'd brushed her off, assuming it was wishful thinking on her part.

It also stood to reason that if Cindy had known about the impending proposal, Thomas had as well, which was probably why he'd felt it necessary to discuss a prenup with Chance later in the week.

Even Amanda had called me her sister a few times throughout the week, which I'd thought was just her being kind.

"Did everyone know?"

Amanda nodded her head, light laughter on her lips. "He was supposed to ask you on Christmas Eve with that whole adorable setup he'd worked on in the atrium, but then you had to go and find a secret room that had been hidden for decades, which resulted in a quick change of plans."

"I rather liked how he proposed on Christmas Day," I replied wistfully, thinking back to all the sweet things he'd said to me as we'd made our way back down to Mitzi and Sasha's room.

"You said yes." Amanda beamed at me. "That's all that matters."

I smiled back at her, thinking the same. "Who knows? Maybe it'll be you next."

Her grin widened, a spark of mischief in her eyes.

"What?" I asked.

"Hiram and I eloped last spring."

My mouth popped open in shock. "Do your parents know!?"

"I told Mom right after."

"But your dad…"

Amanda shrugged. "We'll fake an engagement and big wedding just for fun someday, but for now it's nice to just have something for us."

I shook my head, smiling back at her. "Good for you."

"That dress makes you look badass." Chance grinned from ear to ear as he walked a circle around me, examining every angle of the garment.

I didn't think it was possible for him to look more handsome, but there he was, in a black suit, paired with a black shirt and tie, my perfect match, looking like he'd walked out of a fashion magazine. I'd have to tell him that later, when we were alone, just to see what naughty things he'd say in response.

"I especially like this." His smirk turned sinister as he ran his finger along the exposed flesh of my thigh, thanks to the slit.

"Hands off in public, you letch." I swatted his hand away.

He barked a laugh, loving that he'd gotten a rise out of me, the blush on my cheeks evidence of his effect on me.

But he was right, I did feel badass in the dress, with its gilded armor-like shoulder detailing. It struck me how different this dress felt from the black velvet gown I'd borrowed from Amanda the year before. I still loved that dress and often admired it in my closet, but that one was so much more demure. This gown made a statement: that I was my own person and that I was here to stay, whether the crowd downstairs liked it or not.

"When are you guys coming out to visit us?" Amanda asked, straightening Hiram's bowtie for him. He stood tall and proud, his eyes never leaving her as she fussed over him.

"Sooner rather than later," I told her. "Chance finally agreed to get a dog!"

He shook his head. "I agreed we could start looking at shelters to find the *right* dog."

"Same difference." I waved my hand, dismissing his clarification.

Amanda shook her head at her brother, her smile showing her amusement.

Walking down the grand staircase for this one last event, arm in arm with Chance, felt different than the others I'd attended the week before. Hell, it felt like the Revelry had happened months ago, not a mere week.

Of course, the fact that Chance and I had gotten to spend the week in between lost in bed with one another, celebrating our engagement, would make anyone feel a little discombobulated.

Over the evening, I was surprised at all the people who approached us with congratulations on the engagement. I was sure it had more to do with keeping up with appearances and making sure their relationships with Thomas and Cindy remained intact, but it felt good to be seen by them as more than a transient part of Chance's life.

I was proud of myself for being able to hold my own, even if it was because Chance was at my side. His unwavering support and love gave me the confidence I needed to become a new version of myself...one that had a thicker skin and knew herself enough to not be bothered with others' opinions. I couldn't change where I'd come from, but I absolutely had a say in my future.

"I don't think I'm going to make it to midnight," Chance whispered in my ear around ten, his fingers playing at the slit of my dress. "Think we can sneak out a little early?"

"We never did get to use the giant bathtub in your room..." I replied suggestively.

A smile curled the edge of his lips.

Chance's hands were all over me the second his bedroom door closed behind us.

"Don't rip the dress," I panted between kisses as his fingers tore at the belt at my waist, then the zipper at the back, while I made myself busy unbuckling his pants.

"I'll buy you a new one," he quipped, shoving the sleeves down my arms, the dress pooling at my feet a moment later. Without another word, he picked me up, our bare chests meeting, and carried me to the bed.

"Can't wait—won't be gentle," he huffed, setting me down at the foot of the bed.

"You should know by now you can have me any way you want me," I simpered, looking up at him through my lashes before sliding my panties down my legs, baring myself to Chance completely.

"Turn around," he commanded.

I obliged.

I felt his warm hand at the center of my back a moment later, gently indicating he wanted me to bend over the bed. And then his cock was sliding against my already wet core, teasing me with slow strokes. "I thought you weren't going to be gentle," I sassed, arching my back so my ass was higher in the air.

"Well, if you're going to be a brat, maybe I'll just edge you for the rest of the night," he whispered, leaning over me, his chest against my back.

I whimpered at the thought.

"Will you be a good girl?"

I nodded, my cheek resting against the duvet.

With a single stroke, he entered me.

We each released a synchronous low groan.

"Nobody could keep their eyes off you tonight," Chance crooned in my ear as he slowly rolled his hips against me. "But you only had eyes for me, didn't you, muse." The question was said as a statement of fact.

"Only you…" I whimpered, drowning in the feeling of fullness he provided while he was inside me.

"They all want what they can't have," he growled, his voice low and husky as his lips grazed my ear. "Because they know you're mine."

"Yours…" I moaned, relishing that his thrusts were slowly picking up speed. This version of Chance, who was possessive and obsessive, only came out in the bedroom.

He was so calm on the surface, so easygoing around everyone else. But when it was just us, he let me see who he really was…a man who was desperate for what belonged to him…me…

"Will you beg me, baby?" he murmured, his lips trailing down my spine.

"Please…please, Chance," I pleaded. "I need you…I need this."

His speed increased, and I felt my own climax within reach.

As if sensing its approach, Chance reached around my hip, easily finding my clit and providing the pressure and friction I needed to soar. I released a strangled cry as my orgasm hit, my fingers digging into the bedding as his pace became more erratic.

Only a moment later, Chance cried out when he found his own release, collapsing on top of me, still buried inside, our breathing in sync as we came down from the high.

"Amanda told me she and Hiram got married in secret months ago," I gossiped with Chance from across the bathtub, where we'd decided to ring in the new year.

His eyes shot up from the foot he was massaging for me to cast me a guilty look.

"You knew!?" My eyes widened. "Alexander Chance Harper, shame on you!"

He chuckled at my bombastic response.

"She said she wanted to tell you herself, and if you think you're scary when someone crosses you...well, you haven't seen Amanda scorned." He set my foot down and grabbed the other, sliding his thumb along the arch.

I threw my head back, enraptured with his touch. The shoes Amanda had procured weren't as bad as I'd assumed they'd be, but having to stand in even the most comfortable pair of heels for a few hours was bound to take its toll.

"You like that?" Chance said suggestively, digging in deeper to my arch.

I could only groan in response.

"Thank you for coming with me tonight." His tone became more reverent.

I glanced at him through half-closed lids, my breath deep from the relaxation of his massage and the aromatic warm water that enveloped us both in the giant bathtub in his ensuite. "I don't mind, as long as I'm with you." I gave him a soft smile, which he returned.

"Me too."

"I actually had a good night," I expanded. "It's funny, but now that I finally feel like I've found my place, I've realized you were right all along."

Chance raised an eyebrow—always happy to hear me tell him when he was right.

"I don't need their acceptance. I don't need their approval. I don't care about their opinions. I only care about the people who matter most to me," I clarified. "As long as we have each other, I won't need anything else."

"Violet Price, are you going soft on me?" Chance leaned forward in the tub, water sloshing around him with the sudden movement.

"Never." I grinned at him.

Chance kissed me softly, one hand winding into the hair at the base of my neck. "Good, because I want you just as you are."

And for the first time in a long time, I believed that I was enough.

THANK YOU

Thank you for reading *Last Chance Christmas*!

If you enjoyed the book, it would mean the world to me if you would consider leaving a rating or review on Amazon, Goodreads, or the platform of your choice.

ACKNOWLEDGEMENTS

I don't quite know where to begin.

Do I start with how incredible the last year has been because of *The Other Side*, or the huge amount of people that contributed to the making of this book, or just how much I didn't realize that I needed to revisit Chance and Violet one last time?

I suppose I'll just start from the beginning.

Of course when you write a book you hope that it will connect with people. Chance and Violet had been following me around for over a decade by the time I published *The Other Side* and the version that was published was so much of me that I couldn't have dreamed that it would resonate with people like it did, or that readers would share it with their friends, or drop into my DMs to say they appreciated Violet's struggle with anxiety so much, or that it would lead to opportunities beyond my wildest dreams. I simply had a story to tell and characters that I needed to give voice to.

So when the book was out and done and I saw how much people enjoyed it, there were a few people that reached out asking if I planned for more. And I hadn't...initially. But while talking to someone over DMs (shout out to Makayla!), when she asked if

Chance and Violet would ever be back, I jokingly said, hey, you never know, maybe a holiday novella someday. And immediately the ideas started pouring into my head. Of course it had to be at his parent's mansion, and obviously they'd need another mystery to solve. But they'd been through so much in their first book, so I wanted to keep it lighter. And I thought, what's better than following clues and going on a treasure hunt to solve a mystery your ancestor left behind? And because I love a good pun, I thought it would be funny to have Chance's name in the title and again jokingly titled it *Last Chance Christmas* thinking I would change it later, but then it just kind of stuck.

The words just flowed out of me, and these characters practically wrote themselves. Every little detail fit into place, even things I hadn't planned on! While brainstorming nicknames for Chance's grandfather so I could have the big reveal at the end, I found that Sasha was a nickname for Alexander and couldn't believe my luck. I thought Chance, being the cheeky man that he is would think it would be funny to give Violet a violet engagement ring and when I was researching purple and violet gemstones, I was shocked to find the one I was drawn to (Alexandrite) somehow had a very particular link to Russian nobility, which so perfectly dovetailed into Sasha and Mitzi's story. From the moment I started envisioning this book, it felt like the universe conspired to let it happen, even though I originally never planned to revisit Chance and Violet again.

I didn't realize until the final draft of the book had been completed how much I needed this book. The novel I'd written right before this (which I plan on publishing next year) was easily the hardest book I'd ever written, and at times had me questioning if I'd lost my magic or maybe if I was putting too much pressure on myself and was just burnt out. But no...it was just a tough book, and I can still write, and I learned a lot of lessons along the way, like to lean into the pieces of the characters that are a part of me. Writing this book was healing in so many ways, and I'm so thankful that it was because of my readers that it even happened.

Now onto the fun bit, where I get to thank the incredible people that helped me along the way with this fun, schmoopy, little holiday romance. Because it's easiest, I'd like to go in order of their assistance in my process.

First I'd like to thank the regulars, my family (especially my mom, HI MOM!), my best friend Caitlin (thank you for always being the best captive audience even though I know you have no interest in reading any of my books, you always let me talk your ear off), my Saturday writing group, the Monday night yoga crew, including my lovely friend Amanda, for whom Chance's sister is named after, and thank you Amanda, for letting me name her partner after yours: Hiram! It felt only right that the two of you should be together on the page as well. And congratulations on your recent nuptials and all the amazing new developments in your life!

Thank you to Heather, the first reader of all my books who gives me a positive, yet critical lens to make my work stronger. To my beta reading team (LL, Courtney, Adrienne, Caitlyn, Emma, Melissa, McKenzie, and Kelsey), which was a bit larger for this book because I needed to make sure a) I wasn't imagining that I liked it, and b) that it would be enjoyed by those who both had and had not read

The Other Side, I am so appreciative of your time and thoughtful comments, which also helped immensely with improving the story and characters!

To my copyeditor, Sam, I still feel so incredibly lucky to get to work with you. I love your notes, your infectious enthusiasm over the English language, and all the kind words of support you've offered me since the moment we met. You mentioned when you handed this book back over that you appreciated my unique voice as an author, and I don't think I'd ever felt so flattered in my life that my writing style was somehow distinguishable from others. Thank you.

Emarie, your cheerleading always puts a smile on my face, and you give me the best ideas for unique marketing content and character art. I appreciate all the little emoji comments you leave on my manuscript in between corrections when you're proofreading.

To Sarah, my wonderful PA, who is directly responsible for helping to get *The Other Side* in the hands of so many people, you've been a constant source of support, and I've really enjoyed not only working with you, but also becoming your friend in the last year. I have so much planned, and I can't wait to bring you along for the ride!

Of course I'd be remiss not to thank the lovely artists that have made time to work with me on this book. First, Rachel, the brilliant mind behind the cover. I loved what you created for *The Other Side* so much, I said, let's take it out for one more ride. You're an absolute mind reader and your attention to detail is delightful. And to Sally, who has worked with me to make these characters come alive with your art, I need to start recording reaction videos when you send over your progress emails because I think you'd get a real kick out of my jaw being on the floor and tears welling in my eyes when I see the amount of work and detail you've put in to your art. Thank you also to Maral (fashion sketches), Albino (Harper House illustration), and Termeh Studios (Harper House floorplan), who all contributed their fantastic artwork and services to make this book come alive.

I've also been privileged to have made some new friends in the last year, which I truly believe I never would have met if I hadn't been on this fun publishing journey. To Nancy, Stephanie, Mandi, Tiffany, Allison, Lisa, Freya, Melanie, Lauren & Tina, and the SoCal Story Society, thank you for your kindness and open arms. I'm still working on not being a hermit, but y'all make it easier. Again, the opportunities that all of you have brought my way continue to astonish me, and I am forever grateful for your friendship.

To the women of Heartbound Bookshop: Jenika, Ayesha, and Cecilia, I truly feel I am forever indebted to you. You found me last year, after my debut released, and gave me the honor of gracing your shelves (my first store shelves!), and it felt only right that I release my very first special edition book, exclusively with you. The way you lead with love in everything you do is so admirable and an example I gladly work to follow.

And lastly, but never least are my readers, including the many lovely people that I've connected with on Instagram. I don't think you'll ever understand how much your support has changed my life. You've given me strength to keep writing, when I wasn't sure if I should keep going, you've offered support when I didn't realize

I needed it, and you've shown me that my words matter...that *I* matter, and I will be forever grateful for the time you've taken to read my books and share them. I've had to come up with bigger dreams because you've all made the ones I already had come true!

That's all for now, but I'll be seeing you all very soon, when I return with my next book in 2026: *Radiant Exception*.

Cheers!

ABOUT THE AUTHOR

AJ Wynn is a Southern California-based author who works in marketing professionally, but whose true passion lies in writing. Weaving captivating stories with romance, mystery, fantasy, and much more allows AJ to express her creativity and serves as a canvas for her boundless imagination. When not immersed in the world of words, AJ is an avid reader, book dragon, and interior decorating enthusiast. Her favorite cozy days are accompanied by a fresh cup of coffee and her faithful canine sidekick.

Stay up to date with AJ Wynn's latest releases by subscribing to her newsletter at AJWynn.com or following her on social media @AJWynnWrites.